BIG ROAD WALKER

BIG ROAD WALKER

BY

EULA G. DUNCAN

BASED ON STORIES TOLD BY

ALICE CANNON

ILLUSTRATED BY

FRITZ EICHENBERG

J. B LIPPINCOTT COMPANY

PHILADELPHIA   NEW YORK

CONTENTS

ILLUSTRATIONS

[viii]

FOREWORD

Alice Cannon, from whom I first heard of Big Road Walker, has been cooking for my sister in Winston-Salem, North Carolina, for a number of years. All during her stay there I have been very much intrigued by the tall tales about Big Road Walker and Hokey and their family, with which she has entertained my small nephews and niece, Martin, Sam and Pat. My interest was first aroused when I heard Alice tell the children that Big Road Walker smoked a pipe so big, "till five little boys could set on de rim of it." Obviously Big Road Walker was quite a personage.

The children were always so entranced by these stories that it seemed a pity to me that other children shouldn't have the same enjoyment. Consequently, I made a practice of taking a notebook with me when I went to Winston-Salem, and of jotting down odd bits of information about Big

Road Walker and the others. This past summer I assembled some of my notes, and wrote out the first two chapters of this book. Presuming on friendship, I persuaded the Children's Librarian of The Greensboro Public Library to read them. Her verdict was so encouraging that, on her recommendation, I submitted these two chapters to the Stokes Company, and this book is the result.

Alice, as might be inferred, is from Newberry, South Carolina. She tells me that her father told her stories about these characters when she was a child, and that his father told them to him. I have made numerous inquiries, but I have been unable to find anyone else who is familiar with Big Road Walker and Hokey, so apparently they originated with her grandfather, who must have been a very small boy about the time of The War Between the States.

It is my sincere wish that all the children, and grown-ups too, who read this book, will receive as much pleasure from the stories as have Martin, Sam, Pat and their aunt.

EULA GRIFFIN DUNCAN

Greensboro, North Carolina
January 15, 1940

* 1 *

BIG ROAD WALKER
AND HIS FAMBLY

"You Mahtin!   Git down outen dat chair.   Git down, I say!"

"Ain't going to do it."

"You better git down outen dat chair 'fore ole Hokey knock you down."

"I ain't 'fraid of Hokey.   She's just a little old lady, and can't hurt me."

Crash!

"See now!   I tole you ole Hokey'd knock you down.   I done tole you she don't like bad chilluns."

"Alice, tell us about Hokey, and Big Road Walker, and Iba Diddy, and Crabby Jo May, and Mean O My, and Tuba Labba, and Sizzie Higgins."

"All right, Pat.   If you and Mahtin and Sam

will set down and be good chilluns while I makes out dese biscuits, I'll tell you sumpn 'bout 'em dat I ain't tole you befo'."

You 'member dat Big Road Walker, he de papa, and little ole Hokey, she de mama, and Iba Diddy and Tuba Labba and Crabby Jo May and Mean O My, dey's de chilluns. And Sizzie Higgins, she de cook for dey all, and dey all lived in Newberry, South Cahlina. Mean O My and Crabby Jo May is boys, and Iba Diddy and Tuba Labba is girls. Tuba Labba's 'bout big as you is, Pat. Iba Diddy, she de baby of dey all.

Ole Big Road Walker's de bigges' man dey is. He so big till he's big as dat go-riller ape we see at de circus. He's high as a house, and his legs is so long dat when he take a step he go a mile every time. He's a real black man, wid a roun' face, and de whites' teef. His mouf's as big as a elephant's mouf, and he can swaller a whole hoecake of bread at one bite. He eats twelve hoecakes of bread for brekfus and dinner and supper, every day. He got a nose ten inches long, and his ears is so long dey flops like a ole plow mule's does when he's wukkin'. He got de mos' hair on his haid, and his eyes is big as teacups. He got ten toes on bofe his foots. His hands is big as dis breadboard, and he

[2]

*He so big he has to go in
de store on he knees.*

got leben fingers on 'em. His arms is so long dey come halfway down his legs. When he's jus' wukkin' he wears his overhalls, and he don't wear no shoes and no shirt, but when it's Sunday and he goes to de church-house, he put on his Sunday suit wid de long-tail coat like de preacher. He put on his shoes when he go to de church-house, too.

Big Road Walker's a good man, too, if you don't make him mad, but when he do git mad he turns over houses and pulls up trees, right by de roots.

He's right smaht, too, 'bout wukkin'. He do mos' anything, but mos' times he wuk in de cotton fiel' to git him some money to buy vittles wid. But sometime he don't buy what he want, he jus' go to de groc'ry man's and pick up what he want and go out. He's so big de groc'ry man's skeered to tell him not to. He so big he has to go in de store on he knees, and stay on 'em till he come out. He buys baccy for his ole corncob pipe, though, 'cause he have to smoke dat pipe all de time. Sometime he smoke cornshuck baccy in de pipe. Dat ole pipe is so big till five little boys sets on de rim of it when he's smokin' it in de wintertime, to keep warm. And dey has plenty room to wiggle in, too.

Big Road Walker's wife is name Hokey. She

[4]

so little sometime she can go right thoo a keyhole, 'thout pressin'. But she's a magic woman and can turn herself to a real lady when she want to. She only got seben fingers on her hands, and two toes on her foots.

Hokey likes good chillun, but she sho' don't like bad ones. You 'member how when you been good chillun she comes here, and you can't see her, and she leaves chewin' gum and candy for you. She come in de house, open de door, and nobody don't see her, and she always stan' in de corner, or by de fiahplace. She'll talk to you too, but you can't never see her. She only jus' let you see her shadder. When she hears 'bout bad chillun she goes to dey house and make 'em walk backerds, and fall down. Dey be walkin' long, and fall right down, and dey don't know how come dey do. When dey's extry bad she take 'em to de Underground Pasture, where de bulls is at, and lets de bulls run 'em.

Big Road Walker likes to walk in de woods. He foun' Hokey in de woods one day, and dey got married up, and he built him and her a big ole house, long side de main highway. He made hisself a bed outen a oak tree, 'cause he's so big he has to have a strong bed. Little ole Hokey, she jus' have to have a little pine saplin' bed, she so

[5]

little. She pick up a lot of nice, clean pine straw and made 'em some pillows, and dey all fixed up fine. Big Road Walker has to have iron sheets on his bed, 'cause he's so tough he wears out sheets like us folks has. He can't stretch him out on de bed, so he double hisself up in a knot when he lay down. He say he don't never sleep none, but he lay down, sometime. He don't never sleep, night or day. Reason he don't never sleep none is somebody is like to pass on de road where he don't want nobody passin'.

Dey don't have no washin' tub in dey house 'cause Hokey, she so little, she can't wash in one, and Big Road Walker, he wash in de branch. But dey has two doors in it, one in de front, and one in de back. It sho' is a nice house, and dey has another house, too, down under de groun'. Dey keeps de chillun in de undergroun' house when dey travels and don't want to be bothered wid no chillun.

Soon as dey got de house all builded up, Big Road Walker named hisself Big Road Walker, his own self, on account of his house is by de big road, and he walk on it all de time, in de daytime. In de night-time he walk in de woods.

Big Road Walker has to have lots of vittles, so he fotch him a big ole iron pot to cook up a mess of collard greens and side meat in, 'cause he have to keep his strenth up to keep from bein' all holler inside. When he got dat pot set up and a pine-knot fiah goin' under it, Hokey 'lowed to him dat he'd have to go fin' a cook, 'cause she so little she can't see over de aidge of dat pot, much less cook up dem collard greens in it. So Big Road Walker say he'd go out in de woods and fin' a cook. He say he always fin' what he want out in de woods. He say to Hokey, "I'se got to git out and fin' us a cook, 'cause I sho could use me a mess of collard greens and yams and hoecake, right now."

So Big Road Walker, he start out, and he hunt, and he hunt, and he don't fin' him no cook. It's gittin' late, and he's gittin' mighty hongry, and he's jus' about ready to go home and see can he cook up dem collard greens, hisself, when all of a sudden he see de funnies' lookin' lady he'd ever seed, comin' up down de road. She ain't got a hair on her haid, and she ain't got but one leg, but she could walk jus' as good as anybody. She stop in front of Big Road Walker, and she say to him, she say, "Big Road Walker, here I is. I'se a hunnerd years ole, but I'se spry as fifteen. Les' us git on home, 'cause I got to git dat pot to bilin' if you's goin' to have collard greens and hog jowl for you supper."

Big Road Walker knowed right den dat was de cook he been lookin' for, and he took her up under his arm, and off he went, a mile a step. When he come to dey house by de main highway he set her down, and she say to Hokey, "I'se de cook, Sizzie Higgins."

And Hokey say, real polite, "Light, and make yourself to home."

So Sizzie Higgins, she got de water to bilin', and put some collards and hog jowl in de pot, and some yams in de ashes, and made up a mess of hoecake, and before dey knowed it dere was de bes' supper you ever popped your bill into, jus' waitin' to be et.

Hokey and Big Road Walker 'lowed dat Sizzie Higgins was jus' what dey'd been lookin' for, all de time. Dey tole her dey'd pay her fifty cents a week to stay and cook for 'em, and she say all right, but she ain't goin' to go trav'lin' roun' wid 'em when dey goes on dey long trips, on account of she like to stay home all de time. She tell 'em she don't need no bed to sleep in, on account of she sleep in de corner, standin' up, and she don't never sleep much, nohow.

Hokey and Big Road Walker loves to travel. One time dey went roun' de worl' in three days, and I'm tellin' you, dat was a trip. Dey went from

[8]

Newberry, South Cahlina, right smack to New York, and to St. Louis, Missoury, and back, and it didn't take 'em but three days! One time dey went to De Other Worl', 'cause Hokey's a magic woman, and she can fix it. Dey went to two towns dere. One of 'em name "Don't-Come-Here," but dey come dere, anyhow.

After de chilluns was borned, Big Road Walker made seats all roun' hisself to put de chilluns on, and dey took dem trav'lin' too, but when dey don't take de chilluns wid 'em, Hokey always bring 'em back lots of toys. One time dey was goin on a long ole trip, and when dey was jus' about ready to go Mean O My pushed Crabby Jo May in de fiah and burnt his face. Hokey got so mad she grabbed him by de arm and flang him on de floor so hard he bounced right up to de ceiling. Big Road Walker, he got so mad at him he squeezed his nake little as a needle, and he say to him, he say, "Mean O My, you's a bad boy, and you can't go wid us. You got to go to de Underground Pasture where de bulls is at till we comes back." And he went, and he was sorry, and he didn't never do nothin' like dat again.

* 2 *

BIG ROAD WALKER
KETCHES A LION

Hokey got to go wid Big Road Walker all de time when he go off, 'cause sometime he has a good time, and sometime he has a bad time. But Hokey know all de time when he goin' to have a bad time, and she go wid him, but he tell her not to. She's a magic woman, so when he goin' to have a bad time she can fix it so he don't.

One time Big Road Walker say to her, he say, "I got to go a long way off on some bizness, and you stay here wid de chilluns while I'se gone." And she say, "All right."

So Sizzie Higgins cook him up a lot of vittles and pack up for him to take long for his dinner, and he got his walkin' stick and he start off, jus' steppin' it off, a mile every step. He's havin' de bes' time, lookin' at de flowers and trees, and

[10]

sniffin' de air dat felt so nice and cool to him in de early mornin', and he walk and he walk and he walk, till he's halfway to where he's goin'. Bimeby he felt sumpn ticklin' his nose, and he reach up to knock off de fly he thunk was settin' dere, and it wa'nt no fly at all. It was Hokey, settin' on he nose, jus' as peart as a robin in de springtime. Big Road Walker don't like it 'cause Hokey come wid him when he tell her not to, and he 'low to her, "Dear Wife, I tole you to stay home, and you didn't min' me."

And she say, "Yessir. But I was worried 'bout you 'cause I knowed dis was one time you's goin' to have a bad time." So she disappeared off his nose, and he don't see her no more. He went on off down de road, and she went right wid him, but he don't know dat.

Big Road Walker kep' on walkin' and walkin', till pretty soon he met lots of little animals comin' his way. He stop and ask 'em where dey's goin', and dey says, polite like, "We ain't goin' nowhere but away from dat lion." And he say, "What lion?" and dey jus' say, "Dat lion," and keep on goin'.

A little piece on down de road he met some birds comin' his way, and he stop and say, "How you all dis mornin', and where you goin'?" and dey say, "We ain't goin' nowhere but away from dat lion." And he say, "What lion?" and dey jus' say, "Dat lion," and keep on goin'.

Big Road Walker thought dey was all doin' mighty funny, but he kep' on goin' down de road. Bimeby he met a yaller cow and a little yaller calf comin' his way, and he say, "Howdy, Mis' Cow. Where you all goin' in such a hurry?" And she say, "We ain't goin' nowhere but away from dat lion." And he say, "What lion?" and she jus' say, "Dat lion," and keep on goin'.

Big Road Walker thunk dat was a lot of puzzlement to be goin' on roun' de woods, and he say to hisself, "Mus' be some ole lion to git all dem animals riled up like dat. Maybe I better go see 'bout dat lion."

So he kep' on goin' till he met a fox comin' his way, and he say to de fox like he do to de little animals, and to de birds, and to Mis' Cow, and de fox say to him like dey did. Big Road Walker ask him where at is dat ole lion, and de fox tole him he's in he den, down de road Big Road Walker's on. So Big Road Walker 'lowed to hisself he'd go git dat lion and make hisself a nice fur rug for his house. And off he went, lickety-split, and Hokey right wid him, but Big Road Walker don't know dat.

Big Road Walker galloped on down dat road

till he come to de place where de fox say de lion be at, but he don't see no lion, and he don't hear no lion. He go to lookin' roun', and first thing he know he's right up in de mouf of dat ole lion's den, and de lion's inside, takin' him a nap.

Big Road Walker don't think he's skeered of nothin', so he walk up to de lion's den, and he say, real loud, "Come out of dere, Mr. Lion, 'cause I'se goin' to kill you and take you hide for a rug."

Dat ole lion open up one eye and look to Big Road Walker, and he say, "Go 'way and leave me 'lone. I got no time to be messin' wid you." And he shut back dat eye and go to sleep again.

When Mr. Lion don't pay him no mind, Big Road Walker was plenty outdone, and he tooken his walkin' stick and whacked him on de head wid it. Dat made de ole lion mad, and he start to roarin'. When he roar it sound like thunder in de mountains, he roar so loud. Den he start gittin' up, and Big Road Walker look and look, and he thunk he sho' is gittin' in a tight place, 'cause dat lion is bigger dan Big Road Walker is! And let me tell you, dat was *some* lion!

Ole Mr. Lion, he roar and he roar, and den he make for Big Road Walker. Big Road Walker don't know what he's goin' to do, 'cause he don't have nothin' but his walkin' stick to fight wid, and he can't run, 'cause de lion's 'tween him and de road. So he say, "Please, Mr. Lion, I was only jus' jokin' 'bout dat rug. I jus' come long to tell you 'Howdy,' and to pass de time o' day wid you. It's a mighty nice day for you nap, and I'se right sorry I woked you up from it. And now I guess I'll be goin' on my way, on account of it's a mighty long way to where I got to go."

Mr. Lion, he roar some more and keep on comin', and he say, "It ain't very far to where you goin', 'cause I goin' to eat you right now." And he let out another roar and open his mouf ready to eat Big Road Walker, and he can't git it shet again! Dere he stood wid de foolishest look on he face you ever see on anybody. Den he try to step up closer, and he can't move his foots. He so s'prised he can't say nothin'.

Big Road Walker look to de lion to see how come he can't git his mouf shet and can't move his foots, and dere was Hokey, settin' on dat lion's back, workin' her magic on him, hard as she could. She tell Big Road Walker to tie de lion's tail in a knot, and to knock his brain out wid his walkin' stick, and he done it. Den he tied Mr. Lion's tail on his walkin' stick, and dey was ready to come back and git dat lion to make a rug, when he come back from his trip.

An' dere was Hokey, settin' on dat lion's back, workin' her magic on him.

Dat was one time when Big Road Walker was plenty skeered, and he 'lowed to Hokey, his wife, "Dear Wife, I thank you dat you come wid me after I tole you not to, 'cause I don't 'magine I could have ruled dat lion."

And dey went on and finished dey trip, and Hokey went too. And Big Road Walker don't never tell Hokey to stay home wid de chilluns no more.

* 3 *

BIG ROAD WALKER
KETCHES A PANTER

One night Big Road Walker was walkin' in de woods, jus' to be walkin'. He don't go walkin' for nothin' special. Jus' went to be walkin'. He's walkin' long, smokin' he old corncob pipe, filled up wid some good ole cornshuck baccy, and mindin' his own bizness, when he heared a panter hollerin', right peart-like. Big Road Walker say to hisself, "Dat ole panter makin' a awful lot of fuss roun' here, and I reckon maybe I better go make him stop. I don't like no such fussin' in dese woods when I'se walkin' in de woods at night."

So he kep' on goin' till he come up on dat ole panter standin' behine a tree, hollerin' at de moon. He all de time have to holler at de moon when it's a full moon.

Big Road Walker say to dat ole panter, "Mr. Panter, you better shet you big mouf. You makin' too much fuss roun' here, and I don't like no such racket in dese here woods when I'se walkin' in de woods at night."

And dat ole panter jus' laugh and laugh, and say he ain't goin' to shet up he mouf. Big Road Walker tell dat panter another time to shet up he fuss, dat he goin' to ketch him iffn he don't, and dat ole panter, he jus' laugh some more, and say he ain't goin' to shet up. He say dem woods don't b'long to Big Road Walker no more dan dey does to him, and he goin' to make all de fuss he want to. He say he got to holler at de moon when it a full moon like it is.

When Mr. Panter don't shet up when Big Road Walker tell him to, it make Big Road Walker hoppin' mad, and he turn roun' and go home to he wife, Hokey, jus' a'trottin'. When he got to dey house he call to Hokey, and he say, "Ole lady, dey's a panter out in de woods behine a tree, hollerin' at de moon, and he don't shet his mouf when I tell him to. I goin' to ketch me dat panter, tonight." And Hokey say, "How you goin' to do dat?" And Big Road Walker say, "I don't know how I goin' to ketch dat panter, but I goin' to ketch him."

"Look out, Mr. Panter. Here I come.
I sho' goin' to ketch you dis time."

Hokey say to him, "You know dem cotton pickin' sheets we puts on de groun' to put de cotton in when we's pickin' cotton in de fiel'?" And Big Road Walker say he do. Den she say, "Well, I'll sew four of dem sheets together and make a sack outen 'em, and you can take de sack and drap it over de panter's head. Den he can't see you, and you can tie him up good fashion, and bring him on home."

Big Road Walker 'low dat's a good idea. So Hokey take dem cotton pickin' sheets and sew four of 'em together, good and tight, and Big Road Walker took dat sack and went back to where de panter is, and he still standin' dere, hollerin' at de moon. Big Road Walker crope up behine him, and he say, "Look out, Mr. Panter. Here I come. I guess you'll stop you fuss now, 'cause I sho' goin' to ketch you dis time."

Dat ole panter jus' laugh and laugh, and he say, "You can't ketch me, Big Road Walker, and I goin' to make jus' as much fuss as I wants to. Dese here woods is mine jus' as much as dey's yourn. You can't ketch me."

Big Road Walker thowed dat sack made outen cotton pickin' sheets in de air, aimin' for it to fall over dat ole panter's head, but you know what dat panter done? He give a jump and landed way off from where he were, and dat sack didn't land on nothin' but some gallberry bushes and briers. Dat ole panter jus' laugh and laugh, and he say, "You can't ketch me, and I goin' to make jus' as much fuss as I wants to. You don't own dese here woods no more dan I does."

Big Road Walker, he so outdone at dat ole panter not gittin' ketched, he jus' turn roun' and go home to Hokey, fas' as he can go.

Hokey hear him comin' and she holler to him, "Come roun' here, Big Road Walker. I got a nice strong piece of plow line to tie dat panter up wid. You bring him roun' here under dis tree." And Big Road Walker got to tell her he ain't got no panter!

Hokey, she jus' outdone, and she say, "How come you ain't got no panter? Didn't you do like I tole you to?"

Big Road Walker say, "Yes, ma'am. I done jus' like you say, but when I tole dat panter I'se goin' to ketch him, he jus' jump away from me when I thowed dat sack to go over he head."

Hokey tole Big Road Walker he ought to know better dan to tell dat ole panter he goin' to ketch him. She say, "You ought to jus' crope up behine dat panter and drap dat sack over he haid, and don't let him hear you. 'Course ain't no panter goin' to stan' still and let you drap a sack over he haid! Look like you'd knowed better dan dat. You go on back and fin' dat ole panter again, and don't you let him hear you comin', neither."

So Big Road Walker, he took dat sack made outen cotton pickin' sheets and start off again, and dis time when he get to de tree where de panter's at, he don't make no noise at all. He jus' crope up, still as a fiel' mouse, till he got right up behine dat panter. Dat panter's jus' standin' dere laughin' and laughin', and sayin' to hisself, "Dat Big Road Walker thunk he goin' to ketch me. He jus' crazy in he haid. He ain't nothin' but a big ole bag of wind, nohow, and he don't know no better dan to tell somebody when he aiming to drap a sack over he haid to ketch him. He sho' is foolish."

When Big Road Walker heared what dat panter say he got so mad he plum' forgot to be quiet any more, and he jump out at dat panter and thowed dat sack made outen cotton pickin' sheets, hard as he could. He thowed it so hard he done got all tangled up in it hisself, and down he come in de gallberry bushes and briers 'stead of de panter. And de panter, he jus' laugh and laugh and he say, "You ain't goin' to ketch me. I goin' to make all de fuss I wants to in dese woods. Dese woods don't b'long to you no more dan dey does to me. Come to think of it, I b'lieve I'll ketch you, 'stead of you ketchin' me."

Dat panter, he made out to jump on Big Road Walker's back, and him still kickin' roun' in dat sack made outen cotton pickin' sheets. 'Bout dat time, here come Hokey down de road, jus' a'bilin', she's dat mad. She say to Big Road Walker, she say, "I might a'knowed you'd git ketched 'stead of you ketchin' dat panter, so I come long to git you straight."

After Hokey tole dat to Big Road Walker she magicked dat ole panter so dat when he was jumpin' on Big Road Walker de top of dat sack come open, and Big Road Walker got out, and de panter got in. You ought to heared dat panter squall and holler when he got ketched!

Hokey tell Big Road Walker to see did he know how to git dat panter home, now dat she'd ketched him. Big Road Walker don't say nothin', but he tied dat panter up, good and tight, in dem cotton pickin' sheets, and he drug him part of de way, and he toted him part of de way, till dey got to dey house, and dat panter jus' squallin' and hollerin'.

When dey got to dey house Big Road Walker say, "Hokey, dat sho' is a good ole panter we

[23]

ketched, ain't it?" And Hokey, she don't say nothin'.

Big Road Walker tied dat panter to a tree wid dat nice strong piece of plow line Hokey had, and dey kep' him dere till dey builded a log house to keep him in. After dey got de log house builded for de panter, Big Road Walker say, "Dat such a spunky panter, I b'lieve I tame him up and make a pet outen him." And Hokey say dat was all right.

While dey's waitin' for dat panter to tame up, dey got to feed him what he like, and dat panter don't like reg'lar food. He jus' likes raw meat, cows, and things like dat, fresh. And he such a mean ole panter he won't let nobody feed him, 'cep' Hokey, 'cause she's a magic woman, and she ain't skeered of him.

So Big Road Walker, he has to go out in folkses pastures and ketch dere cows, and pull dere necks off, and skin 'em for dat ole panter, till he got him tamed up. Dat was a heap of trouble to do dat, and Mr. Panter weren't gittin' no tamer, and Hokey, she gittin' tired of all de time havin' to feed him, 'cause he won't let nobody else feed him. Big Road Walker say he got to do sumpn to git dat ole panter tamed up in a hurry, but he don't know how to do it.

Hokey say to him, "You do like I tell you to do, and we git dat panter tame up quick," and he say he will. Den she say, "You go down to de Underground Pasture where we keeps de bulls, and ketch a black bull, and kill him and bring him back here."

So Big Road Walker went to de Underground Pasture, and he ketched him a big black bull, and brang him back to where Hokey is.

Den Hokey say, "Now you got to draw de blood outen dat bull." And Big Road Walker drawed de blood outen de bull.

Den Hokey say, "Now you got to spit in dat blood, and give it to de panter." And Big Road Walker spitted in de blood and give it to de panter, and dat panter was tame as he could be. Dey didn't have to do dat but one time befo' dat panter was jus' as tame as a kitten, and dey keep him in de house to min' de chilluns when dey's away.

De chilluns is all so proud of dat ole panter dey name him Grandfather.

⋆ 4 ⋆

BLACK BOTTOM

After Hokey and Big Road Walker got Mr. Panter all tame up, and de chilluns call him Grandfather, he don't have to have fresh meat to eat all de time, and he let somebody else feed him but Hokey. When he don't have to have fresh meat to eat he special diet is live snakes, and he like a nice spread adder bes' of all. Big Road Walker go down to de new groun' two times every day and ketch him a nice spread adder off'n stumps for him to eat.

One day Big Road Walker went down to de new groun' to ketch a snake for dat panter, and he look and he look and he look, but he can't find no snake. He see he done ketched all de snakes dat was in dat new groun', and he don't know what to do. So he go back home to Hokey, and he say to her, he say, "Hokey, I done ketched all de snakes in de new groun', and I don't know where to git any more snakes for Grandfather Panter to eat."

Hokey, she say, "Big Road Walker, you know dat bottom lan' we calls Black Bottom, where it so damp and wet, and so many trees is?" And Big Road Walker say he do. Den she say, "Well, I bet dey's mos' five hunnerd snakes down dere. You better go down to Black Bottom and git a mess of snakes at one time for dat ole panter."

Big Road Walker 'low dat's a good idea, and he say he'd go right on down dere and git a mess of snakes at one time, so Mr. Panter could have one for he supper. He lef' de chillun wid de panter, what dey call Grandfather, and tole him to watch dem young'uns good, and if dey didn't behave deyselves to take a bresh to 'em. And he say he will. And dem young'uns was jus' as good as dey could be dat time, and Grandfather Panter didn't have to take no bresh to 'em.

Big Road Walker got a poke and slang it on his back, and he got he walkin' stick, and off he went, a mile every step, down to Black Bottom to git a mess of snakes for de panter. When he got down in de Black Bottom he looked roun', and he see de mos' snakes he ever see. Dey was spread adders on every stump, and he say to hisself, "Ole Hokey sho' tole me right. I bet dey's mos' five hunnerd snakes down here, and mos' of all is spread adders like ole Grandfather Panter like. Dat ole panter goin' to be glad I come down here to git all dese snakes." He was so glad Hokey had tole him to go to de Black Bottom.

Big Road Walker lay down he walkin' stick, and he unslang dat poke from off his back, and he start roun' pickin' up snakes and puttin' 'em in de poke, to take back to de panter.

Bimeby he heared a noise, and he look aroun', and he see de purtiest little black bear behine him. Dat bear had Big Road Walker's walkin' stick in he han', and he's jus' watchin' Big Road Walker pickin' up snakes and put in his poke. When dat little bear seed Big Road Walker, he jus' got right foolish 'bout him, and he followed him everywhere he went down in de Black Bottom.

Big Road Walker don't say nothin' to dat little bear, but he go on pickin' up snakes for Mr. Panter. When he got de poke mos' half full he begin to git tired, and he say to hisself, "I reckon I better res' myself some befo' I gits dis poke full of snakes." And he set down on a stump, and he set de poke wid de snakes in it beside of him. While he was settin' on de stump restin', he look up, and dere was dat little black bear set-

De little black bear say, "I wants
to go home wid you."

tin' right beside him, and he set right dere till Big Road Walker got up and started pickin' up some mo' snakes. And Big Road Walker don't say nothin' to de little bear, and de little bear don't say nothin' to Big Road Walker.

After Big Road Walker got all de snakes he want, he pick up he walkin' stick and start back home, and dat little black bear, he start right behine him. Big Road Walker say to de bear, "Little Bear, you go on back down in Black Bottom and stay. I got to go home now and take dese snakes to Grandfather Panter, on account of dey's his special diet."

But de little bear don't go back to Black Bottom. He say, "I don't want to go back to Black Bottom. I wants to go home wid you."

So Big Road Walker 'low to hisself dat he mought jus' as well take dat little ole black bear home wid him, 'cause he got a panter too, and he already builded a log house for de panter, and de little bear can stay in dere wid de panter. So he say, "All right, little bear, you can go home and stay wid me." De little bear say, "Thank you, Mr. Big Road Walker." And dey went on back to Big Road Walker's house.

When dey got to Big Road Walker's house he took de little bear out to de log house he builded

for de panter, and he say, "Mr. Grandfather
Panter, here is some snakes I brang you from
down in de Black Bottom. And here is some
comp'ny I brang to stay wid you. Dis little black
bear. He can he'p you min' de chilluns when I'se
gone off."

De panter, he say, "Howdy," and de bear, he
say, "Howdy," but de panter don't like de bear,
and de bear don't like de panter. Dey so jealous
of each other to see which one Big Road Walker
like de bes' dat dey fit and dey fit and dey fit. But
de panter whupped him all de time, till de little
bear say he do like de panter tell him to do.

Dey name de little bear Black Bottom, 'cause
dat's where he come from. And Hokey and Big
Road Walker had a panter and a bear for dey pets.

★ 5 ★

I-DON'T-KNOW

Black Bottom so jealous of ole Grandfather Panter dat he say to hisself he goin' to do sumpn to make Big Road Walker like him de bes', but he don't know what he goin' to do.

One day Big Road Walker is gone off on a trip, and Hokey's over to a neighbor lady's house to visit some, and Black Bottom thunk dat's a good time for him to do sumpn' to make Big Road Walker like him de bes'. He snuk away so's de panter and de young'uns can't see him, and he went a long way off to a lady's house, and he stole de lady's baby and brang her home wid him. De baby was only jus' two months ole, and when Big Road Walker come home, Black Bottom tole him he foun' de baby where somebody had thowed her away.

She say to 'em, "You don't harm
me, and I won't harm you."

Big Road Walker was very proud of dat baby, and Black Bottom thunk to hisself dat he knowed Big Road Walker would like him de bes', now. Big Road Walker didn't know whose baby dat was, so he kep' her and raised her up till she got to be six years ole, and she didn't have no name.

When de baby got to be six years ole dey was all settin' roun' de table, eatin' supper, and Big Road Walker ask her what she want to be name. And she say, "I don't know." So dey name her I-Don't-Know. I-Don't-Know was de purtiest chile in de whole worl'. She had hair shinin' like de sun, and eyes like di'mon's, and she's Big Road Walker's heart.

De nex' day after de baby got to be six years ole, and dey name her I-Don't-Know, Big Road Walker took a trip to De Other Worl', and he lef' de baby in care of Black Bottom. Black Bottom say he take good care of her.

Black Bottom knowed dat baby were de extry pet of Big Road Walker, so he thunk he'd do sumpn extry nice for her. He thunk and he thunk, and then he thunk he'd go git dat baby some nice, fresh milk for her to drink. So Black Bottom went and got de drinkin' gourd to git some milk in, and he go off to fin' a cow to milk. He tell I-Don't-Know to set where she is till he come back, and she say she will.

Jus' as soon as Black Bottom got where he can't see I-Don't-Know, she say to herself, she say, "I-Don't-Know, you is six year ole now, so you better git out and do some trav'lin'." So she went in de house and got her Sunday dress, and her Sunday shoes, and some hoecake, and she wropped 'em up, and she went off.

I-Don't-Know walked and walked, till she come to de pasture where some bulls is at. Dey all look to her real mean, but she say to 'em, "You don't harm me, and I won't harm you." And dey didn't harm her.

Den she walk some mo', and she say she goin' to fin' herself another place to live.

I-Don't-Know walked till she come to de river, and some big ole fishes was swimmin' roun' in de water. Dey all look to her real mean, but she say to 'em, "You don't harm me, and I won't harm you." And de fishes don't harm her none. One big ole catfish say, "Little girl, you want to git 'cross de river?" And she say, "Yessir, Mr. Catfish." And he say, "You jump on my back and I'll take you 'cross." So she jump on he back, and he tooken her 'cross de river. When dey got on de other side, she say, "Thank you kindly, Mr. Catfish. I'se much obliged to you."

After dat I-Don't-Know walk some more, a long way. She met a big ole horse, and he look to her real mean, but she say, "Mr. Horse, you don't harm me, and I won't harm you." And he don't harm her none. Den dat big ole horse say to her, "Little girl, would you like to ride down de road a piece on my back? I'se goin' your way." And she say, "Yessir, Mr. Horse. Thank you kindly, sir. I'd be obliged for a lif'."

So de big ole horse got down on he knees, and I-Don't Know got on his back, and he took her down de road a piece, 'bout four miles. Den he stop, and he say, "Dis is where I'se goin' to stop to visit some." And he got down on he knees again, and I-Don't-Know jump down offn his back. When she got offn his back she say, "Thank you kindly, Mr. Horse."

I-Don't-Know started walkin' again, and she walk, and she walk, and she walk. She seed some mens down in de hills, and she say to herself, she say, "I-Don't-Know, if dem mens see you dey goin' to make you go back to Big Road Walker's house 'fore you git all you trav'lin' done." And she dove in de river.

Dem mens see her when she dove in de river,

[36]

and dey say to each other dey b'lieved it were a maremaid what dove in de river. So dey all run down to see de maremaid, but I-Don't-Know was already gone two miles down de river, under de water, when dey got dere.

* 6 *

I-DON'T-KNOW
MEETS SUSIE

After a while I-Don't-Know got out of de river, and she runned up a hill, and she runned down a hill. First thing she know she runned right up in a lady's front yard. She knock on de door of de house, and a big white bull dog come to de door and bark at her. I-Don't-Know look to dat bull dog, and she say, "You don't harm me, and I won't harm you."

I-Don't-Know thunk dat bull dog look like a man wid two big ears, so she say, "Mr. Man Wid Two Big Ears, is de lady of de house to home?"

De big white bull dog say to I-Don't-Know, "No, ma'am. She's down to de spring wid her little girl, Susie. Dey gone to git some water to wash dey clothes in."

I-Don't-Know look inside dat house, and she see

[38]

it a great big house. She say to herself, "I-Don't-Know, it look like dis de place for you to live." Den she say to de bull dog, "My name is I-Don't-Know. I'se a pore little girl and haven't got no clothes to wear, and no shoes to wear. Is you got a place for me to hide here?"

And de bull dog nod de haid to her. He felt so sorry for I-Don't-Know he took he foot and push de door open for her to come in. When she come in he lick her in de face, and he lifted up his front foots and pat her on de back. He so sorry 'cause she ain't got no clothes to wear, and no shoes to wear.

De bull dog leaded I-Don't-Know to a closet, and when she open de door dere was a whole floor full of shoes, jus' her size. She look up side de wall, and she seed a whole lot of purty dresses, jus' her size. I-Don't-Know see all dem purty shoes, and all dem purty dresses, jus' her size, and she say to herself, "I can wear some of dem shoes, and some of dem dresses, I know. I think I'se in a good place now, and maybe I can stay here."

Bimeby Susie and her mama come from de spring. When dey come in de house de bull dog was jus' jumpin' roun'. His name is Jimbo. Susie say to Jimbo, "Jimbo, how come you lookin' so happy? Don't you know sumpn?"

Jimbo shook he head and wink he eye, but he kep' on lookin' up and jumpin' roun', he so glad de little girl is dere.

Susie had a whole lot of clothes and shoes, and some of 'em was too little for her, and some of 'em was jus' right. She keep de clothes and shoes what was too little for her in one closet, and she keep de ones what was jus' right in another closet, but she want to wear all dem clothes and shoes. She got to thinkin' how could she wear all dem clothes and shoes what was too little for her, and then she thunk to herself, "I jus' trim myself off so's I can wear all dem clothes and shoes." So she say to her mama, "Mama, I'se going' in de kitchen and git de butcher knife, and trim off my feet so's I can wear some of dem purty shoes dat's too little for me."

So Susie went in de kitchen and sot down on de floor. She got out de butcher knife, and she start to sharpen it to trim off her feet. When she start to sharpen dat butcher knife, I-Don't-Know heared her, and she start to sing,

> "You can trim you feet,
>   And you can cut you feet,
> But dey's a little girl
>   In de closet, and
> She can wear you shoes."

[40]

Susie jump up and say, "Who doin' dat singin'? I can hear a voice, but I don't see nobody."

Susie look all thoo de house, and she don't fin' nobody singin', so she say, "I don't see nobody. I'se goin' back in de kitchen and git de butcher knife and trim my sides, and trim my legs, and trim my shoulders, so's I can git to wear some of my purty dresses what's too little for me."

So Susie went back to de kitchen and sot down on de floor. She got out de butcher knife and started to sharpen it. When she start to sharpen dat butcher knife I-Don't-Know heared her, and she start to sing,

> *"You can cut you shoulders,*
> *And you can trim you shoulders,*
> *And you can cut you sides,*
> *And you can trim you sides,*
> *But dey's a little girl*
> *In de closet, and*
> *She can wear you dresses."*

Susie hear dat singin', and she jump up off de floor, and she say, "Dey's a little girl doin' dat singin', and I goin' to fin' her." So she start lookin'.

Susie look under de bed, and behine de door. She look in her mama's closet, and she look in her

[41]

papa's closet, but she don't fin' no little girl. Den she look in her closet where she keep her clothes what's jus' right, and she don't fin' no little girl. Den she look in her closet where she keep her clothes what's too little for her, and dere was I-Don't-Know, settin' on a pile of shoes. I-Don't-Know look to her and start to cryin', and she say, "Will you let me stay wid you? I'se a pore little girl, and I ain't got no clothes to wear, and no shoes to wear."

Susie feel so sorry for I-Don't-Know, and she say she be proud to have her stay in her house. And I-Don't-Know say, "Thank you, ma'am. I'se obliged to you."

So Susie took I-Don't-Know by de han' and brang her out of de closet, and give her a bath. Den she put her on some of her clothes what was too little for her, and some of her shoes what was too little for her, wid buttons on 'em. Den she say, "Little girl, what's you name?" And I-Don't-Know say, "I-Don't-Know."

Susie say dat's a funny name, and she say, "My name's Susie, and my dog named Jimbo. What's you papa name?" I-Don't-Know say her papa name Black Bottom. Susie ask her what her grandfather's name is, and I-Don't-Know say her grandfather name Big Road Walker. Den Susie say, "Is

[42]

*"I'se so glad I can stay here wid
you and Susie and Jimbo."*

you got any brothers and sisters?" And I-Don't-Know say, "Yes, ma'am. I got four brothers and sisters. One name Mean O My, and one name Crabby Jo May, and one name Tuba Labba, and one name Iba Diddy. And my mama named Hokey, and we got a cook name Sizzie Higgins, and a bear name Black Bottom, and a panter name Grandfather."

Susie 'lowed dat I-Don't-Know's fambly had de funnies' names she ever heared and she say dey must be furriners.

After Susie give I-Don't-Know a bath, and put her on some of her clothes what was too little for her, and some of her shoes what was too little for her, wid buttons on 'em, she tooken her in de parlor where her mama's at, and tole her, "Mama, dis is I-Don't-Know, what's a pore little girl 'thout no clothes to wear, and no shoes to wear, and I give her some of mine what was too little for me. I found her in my closet, and she goin' to stay wid us."

I-Don't-Know is skeered Susie's mama ain't goin' to let her stay wid 'em, so she bow to her, and she say, polite like, "How is you, ma'am? I hopes you's feelin' peart today."

Susie's mama is real proud to have I-Don't-Know come to dey house to stay, 'cause Susie ain't got no little girl to play wid, and she say to her, "We's real glad to have you stay wid us, little girl. Susie ain't got no little girl to play wid, and you can stay and play wid her and Jimbo, and wear Susie's clothes dat's too little, and her shoes dat's too little."

I-Don't-Know say to her, "Thank you, ma'am. I sho' is obliged to you. I feels sortly funny in dese clothes, though, 'cause I ain't never had such a fine dress, and such shiny shoes wid buttons on 'em, befo'. I'se so glad I can stay here wid you and Susie and Jimbo."

7

BIG ROAD WALKER
GITS MAD

Bimeby Big Road Walker come back from his trip to De Other Worl', and he come home fas' as he can to see his baby, I-Don't-Know. Soon's he got up to de house he started to hollerin' for I-Don't-Know, and she don't answer him. He go in de house, and he see I-Don't-Know ain't in de house. He go out in de yard and look for her, and he don't see no baby.

Black Bottom settin' way off in de corner, and he skeered to deaf. He say to hisself, "Black Bottom, I know Daddy Big Road Walker goin' to kill you 'cause you let dat baby git away." And he start to cry.

Big Road Walker come back in de house, and he see Black Bottom, and he say, "Black Bottom, where's my baby at?" And Black Bottom, he don't say nothin', and he start to bellerin' out loud.

When Big Road Walker see Black Bottom cry he know sumpn's wrong, and he say, "Black Bottom, what's de matter to you? Where's my baby, I-Don't-Know?"

Black Bottom beller some more, and he say, "De baby's gone, and I can't find her."

Den ole Grandfather Panter, he stick he mouf in, and he say, "Uh huh! Iffn you had lef' her in my care she'd 'a been here now, 'stead of runned away and los'."

Big Road Walker, he mighty nigh crazy when he heared dat I-Don't-Know is los', and he runned out of de house, and he look and he look and he look for her, but he don't fin' her. Den he got mad wid Black Bottom, and he got madder and madder and madder. He got so mad wid dat bear 'cause he let I-Don't-Know git lost, dat he runned back home and grabbed dat bear and pulled his nake off. After he pulled his nake off he put Black Bottom on de bed in de spare room, and Black Bottom's eyes was rollin' roun', and he feet was pattin', and he nake was off.

After a while Big Road Walker got to feelin' sorry dat he pulled Black Bottom's nake off, but he don't know what to do 'bout it. He say, "I'se sorry I-Don't-Know is runned away and los', but I'se sorry I pulled Black Bottom's nake off. I reckon maybe he couldn't holp it if de baby runned off." And he set down in de rockin' chair, and he start to cryin' too.

'Bout dat time Hokey come home from de neighbor lady's house, and when she see Big Road Walker settin' dere in his ole rockin' chair, rockin' and bellerin', she say, "Old man, what's de matter to you?"

Big Road Walker bellered some more, and den he say, "Our baby, I-Don't-Know, is done gone, and we can't fin' her." Den he 'lowed to her, "I done pulled Black Bottom's nake off on account of he let her get los'." And Hokey say, "You don't say so." Big Road Walker say, "Yes, ma'am. I done pulled dat bear's nake off, and now I'se sorry I done it, and I can't do nothin' 'bout it."

Hokey was so mad wid Big Road Walker 'cause he pulled Black Bottom's nake off, and she say to him, "I knowed you'd do sumpn iffn I went off. Where at is you put Black Bottom? Is you buried him yet?"

Big Road Walker say, "No, ma'am. I ain't buried him. He ain't daid, yet. I put him on de bed in de spare room when I pulled he nake off. He's layin' dere on de bed wid he eyes rollin', and he feet pattin', and he nake off, but he ain't daid yet."

Hokey see she got to do sumpn, so she say, "I can bring dat bear back alive again, but you got to quit bein' so keerless when I ain't here. I all de time got to be undoin' sumpn you doin'."

Den Hokey go in where Black Bottom is layin' on de bed wid his eyes rollin', and his feet pattin', and his nake off, and she holler to Big Road Walker, "Hesh you bellerin', Big Road Walker, and give me a han' wid dis here bear's nake."

Den her and Big Road Walker got a holt of dat bear, him at his feet, and her at his head, and she say, "Pull," and Big Road Walker pulled, and she pulled, and dey pulled his nake back on his haid. Den Hokey took a spoon and prized Black Bottom's mouf open, and she blowed her breaf down his thoat, three times. Then she wropped her hair 'cross Black Bottom's face, and she say, "Black Bottom, you can come alive again." And he come alive again and set up in bed, and his eyes wa'nt rollin' no more, and his feet wa'nt pattin' no more, and his nake wa'nt off.

Black Bottom say to Hokey, "Thank you, ma'am. I sho' is glad to git my haid back on my nake proper."

★ 8 ★

HOKEY HUNTS FOR
I-DON'T-KNOW

After Hokey got Black Bottom's nake back on he haid, and brang him back alive again, she 'low to Big Road Walker she reckon maybe she better go and fin' I-Don't-Know, 'cause it look like nobody else could. And Big Road Walker say, "Yes, ma'am."

Hokey went 'cross to a neighbor lady's house and say to her, "Good mornin', ma'am. How is you today?" And de neighbor lady say, "Good mornin' to you, Mis' Hokey. I'se feelin' tolable. I hopes you is." Hokey say, "Yes'm. I'se right peart, but dat baby, I-Don't-Know, she done got herself los' dis mornin', and I got to go fin' her. Would you kindly len' me de loan of your ole rabbit huntin' houn', so's he can sniff out which way she went?"

[50]

An' dey pulled Black Bottom's
nake back on his haid.

And de neighbor lady say, "You don't say! Dat baby I-Don't-Know done los' herself! Do tell. Yes, ma'am, you sho' can take my ole rabbit huntin' houn' to sniff out which way she went, and if I do say so myself, as shouldn't, he can fin' anything what's los'. You got to be sure and feed him some corn pone every day, though, 'cause he can't rightly sniff lessn you do."

Hokey tell de lady she'll feed him some corn pone every day, and she take dat ole rabbit huntin' houn' and go back to her house. She tell Sizzie Higgins, dey cook, to fix her up a mess of corn pone in a poke, and her and de ole rabbit huntin' houn' dog start off. Dat ole houn' he put he nose to de groun', and he sniff, and he sniff. Den he bark, and he bark, and he start gallopin' off down de road, de same way I-Don't-Know had went. And Hokey went right long behine him.

Hokey and dat ole rabbit huntin' houn' walked and dey walked and dey walked, till dey come to de pasture where de bulls is at, but on account of Hokey, she a magic woman, dey don't look mean to her. She say, "Mr. Bulls, is you seen a little girl wid hair shinin' like de sun, and eyes like di'-mon's?" And de bulls all say, "Yes, ma'am. We seed her goin' long here right peart. We heared

So Hokey and de ole rabbit huntin'
houn' got on de big ole catfish's back.

her say she's goin' to fin' her a place to live, and she went off dat way to de river."

Hokey say, "Thank you, Mr. Bulls," and her and de ole rabbit huntin' houn' dog go off to de river.

When dey got to de river where de big fishes was swimmin' roun', on account of her bein' a magic woman, dey was real polite to her. She say to de bigges' fish, "Mr. Catfish, is you seen a little girl wid hair shinin' like de sun, and eyes like di'mon's?" And he say, "Yes, ma'am. I seed her. I done tooken her 'cross de river on my back. She sho' were a purty little girl, and when I put her 'cross on de other side of de river I seed her go down de road dat way. Would you and Mr. Dog like to be set on de other side of de river?" And Hokey say, "Yessir, Mr. Catfish. We'd be obliged for a lif'."

So Hokey and de ole rabbit huntin' houn' got on de big ole catfish's back, and he tooken 'em 'cross de river to where he tooken I-Don't-Know, and he sot 'em down. Hokey say to him, "Thank you, Mr. Catfish." And her and de houn' went on down de road like de catfish tell 'em I-Don't-Know went.

After Hokey and de rabbit huntin' houn' dog got down de road a ways, dey met a big ole horse, eatin' grass by de side of de road. Hokey say to him, "Good mornin', Mr. Horse. How is you to-day?" 'Cause Hokey a magic woman, de ole horse is real polite, and he say, "Mornin' to you, ma'am. I hope you is enjoyin' good health." Hokey say, "I ain't so porely, thank you. Is you seen a little girl wid hair shinin' like de sun, and eyes like di'mon's?"

And de ole horse say, "Yes, ma'am, I sho' did. I seed her, and I tooken her down de road 'bout four miles, on my back. Would you like for me to take you on my back to where I set de little girl down?"

Hokey say, "Yessir, Mr. Horse, thank you. I'd be obliged for a lif'." So de ole horse got down on he knees, and Hokey got on he back, and off dey went down de road, wid de rabbit huntin' houn' trottin' long side. When dey went down de road 'bout four miles de ole horse say to Hokey, "Dis is de place where I set de little girl down, and when I see her las' she's headin' for de river over dere." Den he got down on he knees, and Hokey got off, and she say, "Thank you kindly, Mr. Horse," and her and de ole rabbit huntin' houn' headed for de river.

Befo' dey got to de river, Hokey seed some mens down in de hills, and she say to 'em, "Good mornin',

Mr. Mens. Is you seen a little girl wid hair shinin' like de sun, and eyes like di'mon's?" And dey all say, "No, ma'am. We ain't seed no little girl, but we seed a little maremaid what dove in de river and swum across."

Hokey say, "Thank you kindly," and her and de rabbit huntin' houn' dog went lickety-split to de river, 'cause Hokey knowed dat weren't no maremaid what dove in de river. She knowed it were I-Don't-Know.

When dey got to de river Hokey say, "Ole rabbit huntin' houn' dog, put you nose down and sniff out which way dat baby, I-Don't-Know, went, up de river, or down de river."

And dat ole houn' dog put he nose down to de groun', and he sniff and he sniff, and he bark and he bark, and den he took off down de river, and Hokey right behine him. Purty soon dey see a big house wid a big yard in front of it, and Hokey knowed dat were where I-Don't-Know had come.

HOKEY GITS FOOLED

I-Don't-Know is havin' de bes' time at Susie's house, playin' wid her and Jimbo, de big ole white bull dog, and wearin' Susie's clothes and shoes what's too little for her. She say she don't never want to go back to Big Road Walker's house. And Susie and Jimbo and Susie's mama and papa all say dey want her to stay wid dem and be dey little girl.

When I-Don't-Know tell Susie's papa her mama's name is Hokey, Susie's papa know she a magic woman, and he know Hokey goin' to come lookin' for I-Don't-Know, soon as she fin' out she runned away. He knowed Hokey would come right to dey house, too, 'cause she a magic woman, and she can fin' out where her baby went. So he say he's goin' to fool ole Hokey.

Susie's papa sot down and he got de butcher knife and some planks, and he made a little girl what looked jus' like I-Don't-Know look. Her hair was shinin' like de sun, and her eyes is like di'mon's, but it were only a play doll. He put a spring in her back and woun' her up, and he made her eyes roll roun', jus' like I-Don't-Know's eyes roll roun'. Dey put some clothes on de play doll jus' like I-Don't-Know have on when she runned away, and den dey all sot down and waited for Hokey to come.

Bimeby Hokey and de ole rabbit huntin' houn' dog come up to de house, and dey see Susie and Jimbo playin' in de yard. Hokey say to Susie, "Good mornin', Susie. Is you seen a little girl wid hair shinin' like de sun, and eyes like di'mon's?" And Susie say, "Yes, ma'am. I seed her." And Hokey say, "Where she is now?" And Susie say, "She in my house." Den Hokey say, "She my little girl. Would you kindly fotch her out here?" Susie say, "Yes, ma'am," and she go in de house and tell her papa dat Hokey done come for I-Don't-Know.

Susie's papa went and got de play doll he made to look like I-Don't-Know, and Susie took de play doll by de han' and fotch her out to where Hokey's waitin' for I-Don't-Know. She say to Hokey,

"Here is de little girl I seed, and she been stayin' wid us some."

Dat play doll Susie's papa made look so much like I-Don't-Know, dat when Hokey see her she jus' faint, she so glad to see her. When she come to she grab dat play doll and kiss her on de mouf, and de play doll say, "Mama Hokey, where you been so long? Seem like I hasn't seen you in two years, and I jus' been gone two weeks."

Hokey say to de play doll she thunk were I-Don't-Know, she say, "Honey, how come you runned away and got all los'?" And de play doll say, "Mama Hokey, I'se six years ole, and I thunk I better go trav'lin' some, so I come here to Susie's house, and she give me some of her dresses what was too little, and some of her shoes what was too little, wid buttons on 'em."

Den Hokey say to her if she ready to go home, and de play doll say, "Yes, ma'am." So Hokey put dat play doll on her hip, and dey lit out for home, jus' a'trottin', and de old rabbit huntin' houn' dog, he's jus' a'trottin' right long behine 'em. And all de time Hokey don't know no better dan she got I-Don't-Know, 'stead of dat play doll.

When Hokey go back home it don't take long to git back, and when dey got to dey house she say, "I-Don't-Know, you git down and walk up dem doorsteps, so's Big Road Walker can see you. He been so sorry you was gone."

She put dat play doll down, and you know what? Susie's papa done made dat doll so good till she walk up dem steps jus' like she's I-Don't-Know.

Big Road Walker is settin' in his rockin' chair, rockin' and bellerin', 'cause Hokey hadn't come back wid I-Don't-Know. When he see dat play doll comin' up dem steps, he made sure dat were I-Don't-Know come, and he so glad to see her he stopped his bellerin', and he run out to where she was. He grabbed dat doll and thowed her up in de air, he so glad to see her, 'cause he thunk all de time it were I-Don't-Know.

When he thowed dat doll up in de air, one of her eyes come out, and Big Road Walker jus' skeered to deaf, and he stan' dere and holler for Hokey. When Hokey come in de house dere was Big Road Walker holdin' de play doll in one han', and dat loose eye in de other han'.

Hokey let out a screech, and she say, "What you done now, Big Road Walker? Ain't I done had plenty trouble goin' out and lookin' for dat baby for two weeks when she runned away, and bringin' her home, 'thout you bustin' her eyes out soon as I git her here?"

Den Hokey grabbed dat play doll outen Big

*He grabbed dat doll an' thowed her
up in de air, he was so glad to see her.*

Road Walker's han', and when she do, one of her arms come off, and den Hokey see it wa'nt I-Don't-Know at all, but jus' a play doll, and she fainted. She had been so sure dat play doll what Susie's papa had made were I-Don't-Know, dat she didn't even take a good look at her. And dat was one time dat Hokey didn't work her magic hard enough, and she got fooled.

De nex' day Hokey went out de same way she went befo' to fin' I-Don't-Know, but when she got to de house where Susie lived, it was all locked up, and a gennulman tole her dat de folks dat lived dere had all moved away. Hokey and Big Road Walker never did fin' I-Don't-Know no more, and dey was so sorry.

Big Road Walker say he goin' to fin' him another baby, but he ain't foun' one yet.

⋆ 10 ⋆

A TRIP TO BUY CHRISMUS TOYS

One day Big Road Walker think he want some 'simmons, and he say to he wife, Hokey, "Hokey," he say, "I think I go out in de woods and git me a mess of 'simmons." So he go out in de woods to git him some 'simmons.

It were right cole dat day, and Big Road Walker was steppin' long right smart, lookin' for 'simmons. He looked on all de trees he knowed about, and dey weren't no 'simmons nowhere, and all de leaves had done drapped off de trees. So he went on back home, and he say to Hokey, he say, "Hokey, dey ain't no 'simmons on de trees, and all de leaves done drapped offn 'em."

Hokey say, "Is dat a fack? I reckon it mus' be nearly Chrismus, den, and us ain't got no Chrismus toys for de young'uns. I reckon we better be gittin' dem toys 'fore ole Sandy Claws comes and ketches us."

So Hokey called all de young'uns in where dey is, and she say, "Mean O My, what you want for Chrismus?" And Mean O My say, "Mama Hokey, I wants a train to run on a track, wid a whistle."

Den Hokey say, "Crabby Jo May, what you want for Chrismus?" And Crabby Jo May say, "Mama Hokey, I wants a automobile wid red wheels and a yaller top, and a bam-bam horn."

Den Hokey say, "Iba Diddy and Tuba Labba, what you all want for Chrismus?" And Iba Diddy and Tuba Labba say, "Mama Hokey, us wants a big doll wid real hair, what can walk and talk and go to sleep and say 'Mama' and 'Papa.' "

After she ask de young'uns what dey want for Chrismus, she tell 'em to go back to dey playin', and she say to Big Road Walker, "Big Road Walker, I ask de young'uns what dey want for Chrismus, and I reckon we better go to De Other Worl' to git dem toys, on account of none of dese here stores in Newberry, South Cahlina, is got any good enough for dem young'uns. You better go git out our train and polish her up good, and fill her up wid coal, so's we can go to De Other Worl' in style."

And Big Road Walker say he would. He went

out to de shed where dey keep dey train, and it was long as from here to St. Louis, Missoury. De car boxes was dat long, widout de engine, and Big Road Walker made dat train hisself. He wash up dat train, and polish her up good, and fill her up wid coal, and he all ready to go.

Den Big Road Walker go in de house and put on he Sunday suit wid de long-tail coat like de preacher, and Hokey put on her Sunday dress and her Sunday hat. Den she tell Sizzie Higgins, dey cook, dat her and Big Road Walker is goin' to De Other Worl' to git dey young'uns some Chrismus toys, and for Sizzie Higgins to go git dey other cook, But Diddy, to come holp her cook up dey Chrismus dinner while dey gone. Dey always gits But Diddy to come holp Sizzie Higgins when it time to cook Chrismus dinner. And Sizzie Higgins say she will.

After Big Road Walker got de train all ready to go, and Hokey tell Sizzie Higgins 'bout gittin' But Diddy to holp her wid cookin' Chrismus dinner, dey tole ole Grandfather Panter dey goin' to De Other Worl' to git some Chrismus toys for dey young'uns, and dey goin' to leave all de young'uns in his care while dey's gone. And ole Grandfather Panter say he look after 'em till dey git back and if dey didn't behave deyselves, he'd bresh 'em good. And Hokey and Big Road Walker got on dey train, and off dey went, 'bout five hunnerd miles a hour, to De Other Worl'.

Big Road Walker was drivin' dat train, and Hokey was jus' settin' back enjoyin' dat ride. She love to ride on a train de bes' in de worl'.

Bimeby dey come to a little bit of a town, name Don't-Come-Here. Big Road Walker slowed up de train, and he holler back to Hokey, "Is dis de town where we's goin' to git dem Chrismus toys for de young'uns?" And Hokey say dat ain't de town.

Dey driv some more, and bimeby dey come to another town, bigger nor Don't-Come-Here, and Big Road Walker slowed up de train, and he holler back to Hokey, "Is dis de town where we goin' to git dem Chrismus toys for de young'uns?" And Hokey say dat ain't de town. De name of dat town is Notice-What-You're-Doin'.

So Big Road Walker driv on some more, and bimeby dey come to another town, and it's bigger dan Don't-Come-Here and Notice-What-You're-Doin', bofe together, and Big Road Walker make sure dat de town. So he slow up dat train, and he holler back to Hokey, "Is dis de town where we's goin' to git dem Chrismus toys for de young'uns?" And Hokey stick her haid out de winder and dat

*Big Road Walker was drivin' dat
train and Hokey was enjoyin' de ride.*

town name Git-Out-And-Git-Under, and Hokey say, "No, dis ain't de town."

So Big Road Walker driv and driv a long way, and dey don't come to no more towns. Den dey start comin' to a great big town, and Hokey holler to Big Road Walker to slow up dat train, 'cause it look like dis de town where dey goin' to git dey young'uns some Chrismus toys. So Big Road Walker slowed up de train, and Hokey stick her haid out de winder to see what town it is, and dat town name Ban-Tan-You-Tan-A-Week-O'Two-Tans-What's-Dat-It's-No-Tans-Here, and Hokey say dat de town. So dey come in de train station, blowin' dey whistle.

Dey driv de train up under de shed and ask de gennulman dere could dey leave dey train in he shed for a while, and he say dey can. So Hokey and Big Road Walker got out of de train. It had tooken 'em three days and three nights to git to dat town.

Hokey and Big Road Walker hadn't et no brekfus, and dey was feelin' purty needy by dat time, so dey say dey better git 'em some vittles first, and den dey look for de store where dey git dat train for Mean O My, and dat automobile for Crabby Jo May and dem dolls for Tuba Labba and Iba Diddy. So dey come to a big hotel and dey went in and got some po'k chops and yams for dey brekfus, and dey didn't feel so needy den, so dey look for de store to git dem toys.

Ban -Tan - You -Tan - A - Week - O'Two -Tans - What's-Dat-It's-No-Tans-Here is de purtiest town dey ever see. Dey was lots of big ole large tall buildin's dere, and dey was big enough dat Big Road Walker could go inside de doors widout bendin' he knees.

After dey walk down de street a while dey see a big store wid lots of toys in de winders, and dey think dat de store where dey fin' all dem toys dey want. So dey went in de store, and dere was de mostes' toys dey ever see. Dey look and dey look and dey look, and purty soon Big Road Walker see a train jus' like Mean O My want, wid a whistle what blowed, to run on a track, and he put dat train in a poke he brang wid him. Den he look some more, and he fin' de purties' automobile for Crabby Jo May. It had yaller wheels and a red top and a bam-bam horn, and it were big enough dat Crabby Jo May could set in it and ride. Hokey say she reckon Crabby Jo May jus' as soon have yaller wheels as red wheels, and jus' as soon have a red top as a yaller top. So Big Road Walker put dat car in de poke he brang wid him.

While Big Road Walker's gittin' dat train and

dat automobile, Hokey's jus' settin' down, restin' her foots. While she's settin' dere restin' her foots she heared somebody say, "Mama," and she seed two big dolls walkin' to where she is, all dress up in pink silk dresses, wid real hair. When dey got to where she is, dey lied down and shet dey eyes, and Hokey knowed dey was de very dolls dey was lookin' for for Tuba Labba and Iba Diddy.

So Big Road Walker put dem dolls in de poke he brang wid him, and dey went on out of de store. Dey didn't ask nobody how much was de train for Mean O My, how much was de car for Crabby Jo May, how much was de dolls for Tuba Labba and Iba Diddy. Dey jus' put dem toys in de poke what Big Road Walker brang wid him, and walk on out. De store man was so skeered of Big Road Walker 'cause he so big, dat he don't say nothin' to him. He jus' look to him and 'low him to do what he want to do.

After dey got de toys for de young'uns Big Road Walker and Hokey go to another store, and dey got a lot of apples and candy and raisins for de young'uns' Chrismus stockin's, and dey all fixed up 'bout presents for de chilluns. Den Hokey say, "What us goin' to git for presents for Sizzie Higgins and But Diddy and Black Bottom and Grandfather Panter, for dey Chrismus presents?" And Big Road Walker say he don't know.

Den Hokey say, "Dat Sizzie Higgins ain't got a hair on her haid, and she boun' to be powerful cole when it's winter. We git her a hair wig for her haid." So dey went to another store, and dey got de purties' hair wig for Sizzie Higgins' haid.

Den Hokey say, "Dat But Diddy ain't got but two toofs in her haid, and she love to gnaw a ham bone powerful good. We git her some new toofs wid some gol' ones in front." So dey went to a toof dentis' and dey got some new toofs for But Diddy, and tole him to put some gol' ones in front, and he did.

Den Hokey say, "Reckon we jus' git half a ham for dat Black Bottom bear. He jus' love ham de bes' in de worl'." So dey went to another store and got half a ham for Black Bottom, and dey wropped it up all purty wid red ribbon on it, and dey all fixed up for Black Bottom's Chrismus present.

Den Hokey say, "Dat ole Grandfather Panter, he jus' like some nice fresh meat de bes' in de worl', and a good ole rockin' chair to set in and rock when it ain't a moonlight night. We git him a good ole rockin' chair to set in and rock, wid a red cushion, and when we goin' home we git him two wil' hogs so he can have some nice fresh meat." So dey went to another store and got a good ole big rockin' chair, wid a red cushion in it, and dey all fix up wid ole Grandfather Panter's present.

After dat dey had all de Chrismus presents for dey fambly, and dey put 'em on dey train, and den dey all ready to go back home to Newberry, South Cahlina.

* 11 *

BIG ROAD WALKER
KETCHES A MAREMAID

After dey got all dey Chrismus presents put on de train, dey's all tired out, and Big Road Walker thunk he like to go fishin'. So he say to Hokey, "Dear wife, we done got all our Chrismus presents, and we's got a train for Mean O My, and a automobile for Crabby Jo May, and two dolls for Tuba Labba and Iba Diddy, and a hair wig for Sizzie Higgins' haid, and some new toofs for But Diddy, wid some gol' ones in front, and half a ham for Black Bottom, and a good ole rockin' chair for ole Grandfather Panter, and I b'lieve I'll go fishin'."

Hokey jus' laugh and laugh, and she say, "Where at is you goin' fishin'? Dey ain't no branch in dis town." And Big Road Walker say, "Ole lady, dat's how much you know. I reckon I don't need no branch to go fishin'. I reckon dey's a ocean in dis town." And Hokey looked, and sho' nuff, dey was a big ole ocean in dat town. So she say to him, "All right, Big Road Walker, you go fishin', and I'll take a walk roun' dis town and look at de peoples." So she took off one way, and Big Road Walker took off another way.

Hokey walk on down de street and look at de peoples, and dey all looks alike. Dey was all tall and skinny, and dey had long heads and long eyes, and roun' moufs. Hokey's walkin' long, lookin' at de peoples, and she met a lady what stop and say to her, "Mornin', ma'am." And Hokey say, "Mornin' to you, ma'am." And de lady say, "How you feelin' today?" And Hokey say, "Ma'am, I been lookin' for Chrismus toys for my young'uns, and I feels like sumpn sont for and couldn't make it. I feels like I'se greasy and dirty and ragged and stomp barefooted, but I'se roun' here yet." And de lady say, "You don't say. How ole is you, ma'am?" And Hokey say to her, "I'se two hunnerd and two year ole." And de lady say, "Do tell. You cert'nly holds your age well, ma'am." And Hokey say, "Thank you kindly." And she went on walkin' down de street.

All de time Hokey's talkin' to de lady, Big Road Walker be goin' down de road to de ocean. When he goin' down de road he met some mens in de road, and dey stop in front of him and say, "Howdy, Mister." And Big Road Walker, he stop too, and he say, "Howdy, gennulmens." And dey say, "Where you goin' to, Mister?" And Big Road Walker say, "I'se goin' to de ocean to go fishin', thank you kindly." And de mens say, "No, you ain't," real mean like. Big Road Walker say, "How come I ain't goin' fishing' in dat ocean?" And de mens say, "You ain't goin' fishin' in dat ocean 'cause us folks don't 'low no strange mens to go fishin' in our ocean." Big Road Walker say, "I ain't no strange mens. I'se Big Road Walker."

And dem mens say, "Us don't keer who you is. You ain't goin' fishin' in our ocean." And de bigges' one of dem mens pick up a scantlin' from off de groun', and he made for Big Road Walker. Den all de other mens pick up some scantlin's from off de groun', and dey all made for Big Road Walker. Big Road Walker weren't skeered of dem men wid scantlin's, though, 'cause he got his waters on. When anybody got dey waters on can't nobody hurt 'em. Dat mean he fix so he can git de bes' of anybody, and he knowed nobody couldn't hurt him wid scantlin's nor nothin' else.

When de mens seed dat Big Road Walker weren't skeered of 'em, dey knowed he had his waters on, and dey knowed dey couldn't hurt him none, so dey got real polite, and thowed de scantlin's away. And dey say to him, "Mr. Big Road Walker, we didn't mean no harm 'bout sayin' you couldn't go fishin' in our ocean. We be glad to have you fish in our ocean. Iffn you come wid us, we'll take you out in our shad boat we's goin' fishin' in, right now." So Big Road Walker knowed dey'd be all right after dey see he got his waters on, and dey couldn't harm him none. So he went along of 'em to de ocean.

Dem men's had a nice big shad boat in de ocean, so dey put dey nets in de boat, and dey all got in, and Big Road Walker got in, and off dey went. Dey went way out in de middle of de ocean, and dey thowed out dey nets, and dey fished and dey fished and dey fished, but dey didn't ketch nothin'. Bimeby Big Road Walker got tired of not ketchin' no fish, so he layed down in de bottom of de boat to res' some.

He layed down dere in de bottom of de boat restin' till he heared one of de mens say, "I do b'lieve dere is a maremaid."

Big Road Walker always wanted a maremaid to take home wid him, so he jump up and say, "Where at is any maremaid?" And dey say, "Dere she is, right over in front of dis shad boat." And Big Road Walker looked in front of dat boat, and

*Dat little maremaid weren't
skeered of dem mens one bit.*

sho' nuff, dere was a purty little maremaid swimmin' roun' in de water.

Big Road Walker say, "I always wanted me a maremaid to take home wid me, and I goin' to ketch me dis maremaid." De mens all jus' laugh at him and say, "You can't ketch no maremaid." And he say, "I goin' to ketch me dis maremaid."

Den Big Road Walker took one of dem nets and tied it in a loop and swang it roun' he haid three times, and he say, "Net, you go git dat maremaid, 'cause I got to ketch her to take home wid me." Den he swang dat net roun' he haid three more times, and he flang it out, and it landed right on top of dat maremaid's haid. He pull dat ole net tight, and he hauled dat maremaid up to de boat, and he lifted her inside de boat.

Dat little maremaid weren't skeered of dem mens one bit. She just sot up in dat boat as peart like as you please. She look to Big Road Walker, and she say, "Mr. Big Road Walker, does you love to eat fish?" And Big Road Walker say, "No, ma'am. I don't love no fish. I can't stan' fish." And de maremaid say, "You jus' de man I been lookin' for. I been lookin' for a man what don't love to eat fish, and I guess I'll go home to Newberry, South Cahlina, wid you."

De mens pulled in dey nets and put 'em in de

shad boat, and dem and Big Road Walker and de maremaid all went back to de shore.

When dey got to de shore all de folks in town was dere to see de maremaid. One of 'em say to Big Road Walker, "How did you ketch dat maremaid? You looks mighty ole to do anything like dat." Big Road Walker say, "Dat was easy. I can ketch anything I wants to. I'se three hunnerd and ten years ole, but I ketches maremaids good as if I'se jus' sixteen."

Dat maremaid jus' laugh and laugh, and she say, "Huh. I jus' let him ketch me, 'cause I been lookin' for a man what don't love to eat no fish, so I jus' let him ketch me."

Big Road Walker was mighty proud of dat maremaid. He toted her down town and got a big ole tin tub, and filled it up wid water, and he put Mis' Maremaid in it. Den he put de tub on de train and sot down to wait for he wife, Hokey, to come back, so he could show her de maremaid he ketched when he went fishin'.

While he's waitin' for Hokey to come back, he start playin' some tunes on he ole fiddle he brang along wid him on de train, and he say, "Mis' Maremaid, I'se powerful fond of singin'. Can you sing me some songs?" And de maremaid say, "I sho' can, Mr. Big Road Walker. I'se de singinges' pore baby you ever see." Den he say, "Can you sing me some songs while we's waitin' for my wife Hokey to come back so we can go home to our house in Newberry, South Cahlina, and take dese toys we got de young'uns for Chrismus?" And de maremaid say she will.

So Big Road Walker fiddled some tunes, and de maremaid singed to him.

She singed,

> *"Dis ole town is gittin' hanty,*
> *Spooks is goin' to walkin' roun'.*
> *Spooks can't git in dis here shanty,*
> *Spooks can't git on dis here groun'.*
>
> *Ghostes walkin' by dese winders,*
> *Ghostes knockin' on dis door.*
> *Ghostes ridin' on dese cinders,*
> *Ghostes gone, don't come no more."*

When de maremaid finished singin' dat song for Big Road Walker, he 'lowed to her he ain't never heared nobody sing so good. So she say she sing him another song, if he want her to, and he say he do. So she singed,

> *"I loves to gamble, gamble is all I do,*
> *And when I lose my money,*
> *It never makes me blue.*
> *I loves to gamble, gamble to win or lose.*

I gambles every mornin', I gambles every night,
  And if you gamble wid me,
I always treat you right.
I loves to gamble, gamble is all I do.

Bimeby Hokey come back to de train, and she holler to Big Road Walker it's time for dem to git on back to Newberry, South Cahlina. She say she knowed in her bones dem young'uns is bein' mean, and dey'd fit and fit, and ole Grandfather Panter havin' a time tryin' to make 'em behave.

Big Road Walker holler back to her dat he ready to go, but for her to come and see what he ketched when he went fishin' in de ocean. So she come on back where Big Road Walker and de maremaid is, and when she see de maremaid she say, "Humph. You didn't ketch dat maremaid. If you got dat maremaid she jus' let you ketch her." And Big Road Walker say, "Well, I got dat maremaid, anyhow, and she can sing de purties' in de worl', and she's goin' home wid us."

So dey filled up de train wid coal and dey started on back home to Newberry, South Cahlina.

⋆ 12 ⋆

DE TRIP BACK HOME

When dey started dat train back to Newberry, South Cahlina, Hokey 'low she's goin' back and lay down and sleep some, 'cause she hadn't slep' none since dey lef' home.   So she go on in de back of de train and go to sleep.

Big Road Walker was drivin' dat train along, and he got to thinkin'.   He thunk to hisself, "Us is got to git dem wil' hogs for dat panter's Chrismus present, and I bet dey's more wil' hogs de way we didn't come to dis town dan de way we did come.   I b'lieve I go back another way."

So he started dat train down another road, and he driv, and he driv and he driv, but he didn't see no wil' hogs.   Den he driv some more, and first thing he know he see way up in front of dat train some buffaloes, standin' on de track.   Big Road

Walker goin' down dat track mighty fas', and he blowed his whistle, and he blowed his whistle, but dem buffaloes don't move. Dey jus' stan' on de track and don't pay him no min'. Big Road Walker stopped de train, and he hollered out de winder to dem buffaloes to git off de track, but dey jus' stan' dere. He blowed de whistle some more, and dey don't move, so he see he have to go git Hokey to git dem buffaloes off de train track, so's he can go on home.

Big Road Walker go on back and wake Hokey up, and he say, "Dear wife, we's got where we is, and we can't go nowhere else, 'cause dem buffaloes won't git offn de track."

Hokey riz up and she say, "How come dey's buffaloes on de train track? Dey ain't no buffaloes where we is."

And Big Road Walker say, "Yes'm, I knows dat. But we ain't where we is. I come another way on account of I thought maybe we could git dem wil' hogs for ole Grandfather Panter's Chrismus present dis way."

Den Hokey say, "I might 'a knowed you'd git in a picklement iffn I went to sleep. Where at is dem buffaloes?" And he tell her where dey is.

Den Hokey went down to de front of de train, and when she see all dem buffaloes on de train track, she say, "Well, I mought as well git dem buffaloes off de track, right now. Us got to git on back home."

Hokey blowed de whistle and hollered, and all dem buffaloes turned roun' and look to her. Den she thowed up her right han' and say, "Scat, you buffaloes." And dem buffaloes scatted off de train track, and Big Road Walker driv de train on. Hokey can do dat 'cause she's a magic woman, and when she thow up her right han' everybody got to do like she say dem to do.

After dey been ridin' some more, Big Road Walker see some wil' hogs runnin' longside de road, and he stop de train, and him and Hokey got out. Dey walked in de bushes and dey foun' two wil' hogs dey thunk be jus' right for de panter's Chrismus present, so dey went after 'em. Dem hogs didn't have no notion of gittin' ketched, though, so Hokey and Big Road Walker runned 'em and runned 'em and runned 'em, but dey couldn't ketch 'em.

Hokey and Big Road Walker got tired of runnin' dem wil' hogs and not ketchin' any, and Hokey say, "You know what, I bet dat maremaid could sing dem hogs right on dis train, you say she sing so sweet." And Big Road Walker 'low dat he bet she can.

When dem hogs heered dat sweet singin',
dey thow up dey haids to listen.

So Big Road Walker go back to de car box where de maremaid was in her tub wid de water in it, and he say to her, "Miss Maremaid, would you kindly sing to dese wil' hogs so's dey come git on dis train for us to take 'em back to ole Grandfather Panter for he Chrismus present?" And de maremaid say, "Yessir, I sho' will." And she start to sing, real sof' and sweet-like,

> *"I plants corn, I plants corn,*
> *I plants corn all de time.*
> *I feeds wil' hogs, I feeds wil' hogs,*
> *I feeds 'em all de time."*

When dem hogs heared dat sweet singin' dey jus' stop and thow up dey haids to listen. Den dey started gittin' a little closer, and a little closer, and den dey started runnin' and runnin' to fin' out where dat sweet music's comin' from, and first thing you know dem hogs was right up at dat train door. Den Big Road Walker opened de door and dem hogs jus' come right in and sot down in de corner, and dey was all fixed up wid de panter's Chrismus present, on account of de maremaid sung so sweet.

Den Big Road Walker and Hokey had a maremaid and two wil' hogs dey got on dey trip to De Other Worl'.

Bimeby dey come to a town name of You-Better-Look-Out. When dey was mos' pas' dat town dey come to a pasture, and dere was some of de purties' cows you ever see. Big Road Walker say to hisself, "Us ain't got no cows. I b'lieve I git us some."

So he got out and stopped de train and went in de pasture and driv him out two cows, and driv 'em on de train. He didn't put de cows in de car box wid de wil' hogs, though. He put 'em in another car box. And he didn't have to git Hokey to holp him. Dat's one time he got sumpn by hisself.

Den Hokey and Big Road Walker had a maremaid and two wil' hogs and two purty cows dey got on dey trip to De Other Worl'.

Big Road Walker show dem cows to Hokey, and she say, "Dem's nice cows. But you know we's got a panter, and a bear, and a maremaid, and two wil' hogs, but us ain't got no horse. Looks like us ought to have a horse." Big Road Walker say, "Dat is a fack. Us ain't got no horse. Maybe us can git us a horse on dis trip."

After a while, Big Road Walker was drivin' dat train down de road, and he seed some horses, way off. So he stop de train, and he went out to look at dem horses. He see one great big ole black and white horse prancin' roun', and he say, "Dat de very horse we been lookin' for."

Big Road Walker went back to de train and got a rope, and he come back and thowed it over dat big ole black and white horse's haid. Den Hokey come out and hel' de rope while Big Road Walker went back and got a plank. He put one end of de plank on de groun', and one end in de door of one of de car boxes, and dey made dat ole horse walk up dat plank, and right on de train.

So den Big Road Walker and Hokey had a mare-maid and two wil' hogs and two cows and a big ole black and white horse dey got on dey trip to De Other Worl'.

Bimeby, dey was almos' home, and dey didn't have but three more towns to go through. And dey was named And-The-Man and Jeremiah and What-You-Goin'-To-Do-'Bout-It? Big Road Walker was gittin' tired drivin' dat train, and he tole Hokey to drive some. Hokey tole him to go on and lay down, dat she could drive dat train good as he could. She driv some, and he say, "You drivin' fine, wife. Drive on." And she driv on, and he went on back and layed down to git him some res'.

Hokey driv right on thoo And-The-Man, 'cause she don't see nothin' dere she want. Den she driv on to Jeremiah, and when she got dere she see a bull dog wid red eyes she wanted, so she stop de train and go to pick him up. When she go to pick dat bull dog up, she see he's a mean ole dog, and he made at her like he goin' to eat her up. Hokey weren't skeered, though. She jus' thowed up her right han', and den he can't do nothin'. She pick him up and put him on de train, and she say to him, "You big and bad, and you knows everything. You been everywhere, and you done everything, but I got you."

Den Hokey and Big Road Walker had a mare-maid and two wil' hogs, and two purty cows, and a big ole black and white horse, and a bull dog wid red eyes, what dey got on dey trip to De Other Worl'.

⋆ 13 ⋆

HOME AGAIN

Befo' Hokey and Big Road Walker got on de train to go to De Other Worl' to git some Chrismus toys for dey young'uns, dey went out in de woods and builded a big house to put de toys in, so's de young'uns couldn't see dem toys befo' Chrismus day. When dey come on in on de train wid all de toys, and de maremaid, and de two wil' hogs, and de two purty cows, and de big ole black and white horse, and de bull dog wid de red eyes, dey stopped de train where dat house was. And den dey got out and put de toys in dat house, and dey put de maremaid in dat house. But befo' dey went up to de house dey lived in, dey builded a big glass cage in de house where de toys was, and dey filled it up wid water, and dey put de maremaid in de glass cage, and she was so happy. She say she's so glad she come home wid Big Road Walker.

Big Road Walker went out in de woods and fotch a big ole holly tree for dey Chrismus tree, and him and Hokey put two hunnerd candles on it. Den dey put de train for Mean O My, and de automobile for Crabby Jo May, and de dolls for Tuba Labba and Iba Diddy, and de half a ham for Black Bottom, and de big ole rockin' chair wid de red cushion in it and de wil' hogs for Grandfather Panter, and de hair wig for Sizzie Higgins, and de toofs wid gol' in 'em for But Diddy under de tree. And it sho' did look purty.

After dey done dat, dey took de apples and candy and raisins and went up to de house dey live in, 'cause dey's goin' to put some of dem apples and candy and raisins in de young'uns stockin's, and a big red horn. Dey didn't want de young'uns to see de maremaid till Chrismus day.

When dey got up to de house where dey live, all de chilluns come runnin' out to meet 'em, and dey say, "Mama Hokey and Daddy Big Road Walker, what did you bring us from De Other Worl'?" Big Road Walker say, "Is you been good chillun?" And dey don't say nothin'.

Den Big Road Walker say to Grandfather Panter, "Grandfather, has dey been good chilluns while we's away?" And de panter say, "Well, not rightly good, but not rightly bad. Dey fit and dey fit, till I breshed 'em all good and hard, and den dey didn't fight no more. I reckon dey been good plenty for one stick of candy apiece. And me too."

So Big Road Walker give 'em all one stick of candy apiece, but he didn't say nothin' 'bout de toys he brang from De Other Worl'. And you know what? When he's givin' dem young'uns dat candy, he plum forgot all about dat panter, and he didn't give him no candy. Dat ole panter was jus' settin' dere grinnin' and waitin' for he candy, but Big Road Walker didn't give him none. When he didn't git no candy he got so mad he runned out to his house, and he turned it over, and he growled and he growled and he growled.

Hokey wasn't dere at de present time when de panter got so mad, or she'd 'a knowed what was wrong. Big Road Walker called her, real low, and tell her dat Grandfather got so mad he turned he house over, and he's settin' dere growlin' and growlin'. He say he don't know how come dat panter got so mad.

Hokey knowed sumpn was bad wrong, so she go out in de yard where de panter is, and she say, "Grandfather Panter, what's de matter to you?

[92]

*De panter say, "I'se mad 'cause you
brought everybody sumpn 'cept me."*

How come you got mad and turn you house over when ain't nobody bothered you none?"

De panter look to her, and he say, "I'se mad 'cause you brought everybody sumpn 'cept me. When I gits mad, I'se mad."

Den Hokey say, "I got you sumpn, but I ain't had time to give it to you," and de panter say, "Well, be givin' it to me, den." So Hokey slipped roun' de house and down de hill, and got a piece of fresh meat, and give it to de panter.

While dat panter was eatin' dat fresh meat, Big Road Walker say to Hokey, "Hokey," he say, "you ought to make dat panter pollygye wid you for how he done to dat house." And she say, "I will, ole man, jus' as soon as he gits thoo eatin' dis fresh meat."

When de panter got thoo eatin' dat meat, Hokey say to him, "Well, Grandfather, you got to tell Daddy Big Road Walker you's sorry you been so mean." And de panter say, "I won't do it today. I'll do it tomorrow, maybe, 'cause I'm not pleased yet." Hokey say, "How many days do it take you to git pleased?" And de panter say, "I tole you I'll be pleased tomorrow."

"Well," Hokey say, "you goin' to pollygye wid him right now. You ain't goin' to wait till tomorrow. You goin' to min' me." And de panter say,

"Dat's what you think. Dat ain't de way I do it. Dat's de way you do it."

Hokey say, "Well, it look like I got to thow up my right han' again." So she thowed up her right han', and de panter say, "All right, Daddy Big Road Walker. I'se sorry I turned over my house and growled, but I'll fix it right up. But you know you done me wrong for not bringin' me sumpn back, and I kep' you house all de time you was gone. And your young'uns too. And you'll fin' all you things jus' like you lef' em', too."

And Big Road Walker felt sortly sorry he didn't go ahaid and give him a piece of dat fresh meat, right off, 'cause dat was what he wanted.

* 14 *

CHRISMUS DAY

While Big Road Walker and Hokey was gone to De Other Worl' to git de toys for Chrismus for de young'uns, Sizzie Higgins, de cook, and But Diddy, de other cook, dey cooked and cooked de whole time dey was gone, gittin' ready for Chrismus dinner.

Hokey had done tole 'em what she want 'em to cook for Chrismus dinner, but she didn't tell 'em to cook no fruit cake. When Sizzie Higgins and But Diddy got thoo cookin' everything else, Sizzie Higgins say to But Diddy, she say, "But Diddy, you know Hokey ain't tell us to cook no fruit cake, and how is us goin' to have Chrismus dinner proper widout no fruit cake?" And But Diddy say, "Dat is a fack, Sizzie Higgins. Us can't have no dinner widout us has a fruit cake on Chrismus.

I reckon I jus' make us one, 'cause I'se de champion fruit cake maker of de whole worl'." And Sizzie Higgins say, "Do tell. Us sho' got to have a fruit cake for us Chrismus dinner, though."

So But Diddy put on her big ole apron, and tie up her haid good, and she light in and make a fruit cake for dey Chrismus dinner. She say, "Us got to have a big ole fruit cake. I reckon maybe I better make it in dis washin' pot."

So she mix up dat fruit cake in de washin' pot, and she make a big one. When it got done it weighed two hunnerd pounds, and dat was de bes' smellin' fruit cake you ever see. But Diddy and Sizzie Higgins hid dat cake when dey got it cooked, so it be a s'prise for Hokey and Big Road Walker. Dey say it goin' to be a Chrismus present for Hokey and Big Road Walker.

When it got to be de night befo' Chrismus, all de young'uns hung up dey stockin's on de chimbley, and den dey went to bed. When dey all got to sleep Hokey and Big Road Walker lef' ole Grandfather Panter and Black Bottom to watch after de young'uns, and dey went out to de house where dey lef' de toys and de maremaid. Dey trimmed up de big ole Chrismus tree wid de two hunnerd candles on it, and den dey went back to dey house and go to sleep.

Bimeby it got to be Chrismus mornin', and all de young'uns woked up early and runned to see what was in dey stockin's. When dey see all de candy and apples and raisins and nuts, and de big red horns, dey was all so happy. Dey jus' jump and holler and laugh, and have de bigges' time.

After a while Big Road Walker say, "Chilluns, les' us all git in a line and go out to de house we builded in de woods, and see if Sandy Claws lef' us anything out dere."

So dey all got in a line. Big Road Walker got in front, and Mean O My got behine him, and Crabby Jo May got behine him, and Tuba Labba got behine him, and de panter got behine her, and Black Bottom got behine him, and Sizzie Higgins got behine him, and But Diddy got behine her, and Mama Hokey, she come in de back, holdin' de baby, Iba Diddy, by de han'. And dey all marched out to de big house to see did Sandy Claws leave sumpn dere.

Big Road Walker opened de door, and he go in first, and dey all come runnin' behine him. But Diddy slip in and put dat big ole fruit cake on de corner of de table, and she say, "Happy Chrismus to Mr. Big Road Walker. Also to Mis' Hokey." And Big Road Walker and Hokey was very proud

*Dey all marched out to de big house to
see did Sandy Claws leave sumpn dere.*

of dat cake. De chilluns was all so happy, and de panter jus' laugh all over hisself.

Dey all sot on de floor, and Hokey start passin' out de presents. She give Mean O My de big ole train wid de real whistle dat blowed, and he was so happy. He jus' run all over dat house wid dat ole train.

Den she give Crabby Jo May dat automobile wid de yaller wheels and de red top, and de bam-bam horn, and he was so happy. He got in dat automobile and run all roun' dat house, makin' dat bam-bam horn bam.

Den she give Tuba Labba and Iba Diddy dem dolls wid real hair, dat could walk and talk and go to sleep and say "Mama" and "Papa," and dey was so happy. Dey jus' sot on de floor and played wid dem dolls and made 'em say, "Mama" and "Papa."

Den she give Sizzie Higgins dat new hair wig, 'cause she don't have a hair on her haid, and she so happy. She say, "Thank you kindly, ma'am."

Den she give But Diddy dem new toofs wid de gol' ones in front, so she can gnaw a ham bone, and she was so happy. She say to Hokey, "Thank you kindly, Mis' Hokey."

Den she give Black Bottom dat half a ham wropped up wid purty red ribbon, and he was so happy. He say, "Thank you kindly, ma'am. Dis de very thing I like, dis good ole ham."

Den she give ole Grandfather Panter some of dat fresh meat and de big ole rockin' chair wid de red cushion in it, and he was so happy. He say, "Thank you, Mis' Hokey. Dis de very thing I like, dis fresh meat, and dis good ole rockin' chair to set in and rock. But I still got to holler at de moon every other night when it's a full moon." And dey have to take him out in de woods every other night when de moon's full, so's he can holler at de moon jus' de same, when it's a full moon. Dey have to stan' him up behine a tree and let him holler.

After dey had passed out all de presents and litted all dem two hunnerd candles on de Chrismus tree, Big Road Walker pulled dat glass cage out in de middle of de floor, wid de maremaid swimmin' roun' in it. When she see de chilluns de maremaid was very proud of 'em, but de chilluns was skeered of de maremaid till Hokey tell 'em she won't harm 'em none. Dey was all so happy of dey Chrismus presents.

Bimeby it got to be time to eat Chrismus dinner, and Sizzie Higgins and But Diddy had been cookin' all de time Hokey and Big Road Walker was gone, so's dey'd have dat Chrismus dinner. So dey all sot down to eat.

Sizzie Higgins and But Diddy had cooked up de bestes' dinner you ever see. Dey had seven guineas and two chocolate cakes. Dey had a pot of blackberry stew, and ten hams cooked. Dey had two hunnerd and twenty-five pies, and a pot of sallet, and baked sweet potatoes, and three hunnerd and fifty fried slapjacks. And dey all et and et and et.

But de maremaid wouldn't eat none of dat dinner. She say she don't never eat nothin'. She don't have to eat. But while dey's eatin' she sung 'em some Chrismus songs. She singed,

> *"All de angels in Heaven shall sing*
> *On Chrismus Day, on Chrismus Day.*
> *All de peoples on earth shall sing*
> *On Chrismus Day, on Chrismus Day."*

After dat she singed dem another song. She singed,

> *"Up in de chariots*
> *Goin' to take my stan'.*
> *Goin' to fight my sins*
> *Like a nacherl man.*
> *I'm so glad."*

And after dat Chrismus day was over.

* 15 *

DE PICNIC DOWN IN
DE VALLEY

One day de sun was shinin' so purty, and it's so
nice and warm dat Crabby Jo May and Mean O
My and Tuba Labba and Iba Diddy say dey want
to go have a picnic. So Crabby Jo May go in de
house and say to Hokey, he say, "Mama Hokey,
it so nice and warm, and de sun's shinin' so purty,
les' us go on a picnic."

Hokey look out de door, and she see he say right,
so she say dey can go on a picnic. She say, "Dis
is a nice day to go on a picnic. I reckon we can
go Down In De Valley."

Den Hokey go tell Sizzie Higgins to fix up a nice
picnic dinner, and she do. Den dey all got in de
automobile. Big Road Walker got in, and Crabby
Jo May got in. Den Mean O My got in, and Tuba
Labba got in. Den Grandfather Panter got in,

and Black Bottom got in. Den Sizzie Higgins got in de automobile wid de basket wid de dinner in it, and she held de basket in her lap. Den Hokey got in, and she held Iba Diddy, de baby, in her lap, and off dey went, to Down In De Valley.

Down In De Valley wa'nt a very far piece from where dey live, so it don't take 'em long to go. Dat's de purties' place you ever see to have a picnic in.

When dey all got out of de automobile, Hokey and Black Bottom went to fin' a nice place to eat dey dinner. Big Road Walker and Grandfather Panter went to git some wood to make a fiah so's dey could roas' some yams in de ashes. Crabby Jo May and Mean O My went to git some water to bile some coffee, and Tuba Labba and Iba Diddy, dey jus' go runnin' roun', havin' a good time. Sizzie Higgins say she goin' to stay wid dat dinner basket, 'cause she don't want nobody to come steal dat dinner she fixed.

Hokey and Black Bottom look and look, and dat was de purties' place. Dey foun' a nice place under some trees to eat dey dinner, and den dey went and got Sizzie Higgins and de dinner basket, and dey spread out a table cloth. Den dey sot down to wait for Big Road Walker and de panter

And off dey went, to Down In De Valley.

to bring some wood, so's dey could make a fiah and roas' some yams.

Bimeby Big Road Walker and Grandfather Panter come wid some wood, and dey made a fiah and put some yams in de ashes to roas'. Den dey all sot down to wait for Crabby Jo May and Mean O My to bring some water so's dey could bile some coffee.

Dey waited and dey waited and dey waited, but Crabby Jo May and Mean O My didn't come. Dey waited and waited some mo', and still dem boys didn't come. Den Big Road Walker say, "I better go fin' dem boys, 'cause dese yams is almos' done, and us ain't got no coffee bilin' to have wid our dinner." So Big Road Walker went to look for dem boys.

He look and he look, and he can't fin' dem boys. So he go on back and he say, "Hokey, I can't fin' dem boys. Look like you better come hunt too."

So Hokey got up and she start lookin' for dem boys, and purty soon she say, "Dere goes Mean O My behine dat ole big rock. You better go ketch him, Big Road Walker."

Big Road Walker go to git Mean O My, but he so big, and Mean O My so little, he can't git him from behine dat rock. So he holler for Hokey, and Hokey come, jus' a'bilin'. When Mean O

My see she jus' a'bilin', he know he goin' to ketch it sho', so he jump from behine dat rock, and fall down in a ditch and got stuck. Hokey runned over to where he is, and she pull him out of de ditch, and he say, "Mama Hokey, don't let Daddy Big Road Walker whup me dis time. I'll be a good boy all de time now."

But Hokey don't say nothin', and she pull him over to where Big Road Walker is, and Big Road Walker breshed him good and hard, and he say, "You ain't never goin' Down In De Valley wid me no more, nor nowhere else."

Den dey sot Mean O My down under de tree and tol' de panter to watch him, and he say he will, and dey go to look for Crabby Jo May.

Big Road Walker and Hokey looked and looked for Crabby Jo May, but dey don't fin' him. Dey hollered and dey hollered, but he don't holler back to 'em. Den Big Road Walker clum up in a tree and look for him. He looked to de north, and he don't see him. He looked to de souf and he don't see him. He look to de eas', and he don't see him. Den he look to de wes' and he see him. He see him swimmin' in de river wid his clothes on.

Big Road Walker holler to Hokey, "Dat Crabby Jo May's swimmin' in de river wid his clothes on."

Hokey went down to dat river, jus' a'bilin', and

she say to Crabby Jo May, "You come on outen dat river. We's goin' home." And Crabby Jo May say, "No, ma'am. I wants to swim some more," and he didn't come out. Hokey tole him another time to come outen dat river, and he wouldn't come out, and she got so mad she 'bout to bus'. And she say, "I don't like to thow up my han' 'gains' my own chilluns, but dis time I goin' to." So she thowed up her right han', and Crabby Jo May come out of de river, and he know he goin' to ketch it dat time, sho'.

Crabby Jo May retch out he han' and Hokey pull him up on de bank, and she say, "We's goin' home right now, soon as I take you to your papa."

Big Road Walker retch for he belt offn his pants to whup Crabby Jo May wid, he so mad, but Hokey say, "No, you shouldn't whup him wid de belt offn you pants. It too big and too long. You git you a good hick'ry switch."

So Big Road Walker got him a hick'ry switch, and he breshed dat young'un good and hard. Den dey slammed de young'uns in de automobile and went home, and dey was so mad.

Dey didn't have a nice picnic, 'cause Crabby Jo May and Mean O My was so bad. But de panter was real nice. Also Black Bottom. Also Tuba Labba. Also Iba Diddy.

* 16 *

DE UNDERGROUN'
PASTURE

Way down under de groun' in de Undergroun' Pasture is where Big Road Walker keep all his prize bulls, and he got ten thousan' of 'em. Every year when dey goin' to have a Fair, Big Road Walker go down dere on de train he made, wid six hunnerd car boxes on it, wid Hokey, and dey see who goin' to be de worl' champion ketchin' a prize bull to take to de Fair. When Big Road Walker take a prize bull to de Fair, he always git a blue ribbon prize on him, too. Sometime when de young'uns is real mean, dey makes 'em go down in de Undergroun' Pasture where de bulls is at, and let de bulls run 'em till dey be good again.

One time it gittin' 'bout time for de Fair to be, and Big Road Walker say to Hokey, he say, "Dear wife, it's gittin' to be time for de Fair, and us ain't got no prize bull yet to take to de Fair." And Hokey say, "Dat is a fack. Us ain't got no bull out yet. I reckon we better git one right away tonight. It goin' to be a full moon, and we always ketches de bes' ones when it's a full moon."

So dey got some rope and Hokey put on some pants like a man, and dey all got on de train and started off. Big Road Walker and Hokey and all de young'uns and Black Bottom and Grandfather Panter, dey all went off.

Dey go to de Undergroun' Pasture de same way dey go to De Other Worl', but dey don't go so far. Dey go over a mountain, and dey go under a mountain, and dey's dere. Dat Undergroun' Pasture's a funny kind of place. It all foggy and smoky lookin', but de bulls likes it bes' of all, so dey stays dere all de time, and when Big Road Walker want a prize bull to take to de Fair, he got to go to de Undergroun' Pasture to git one.

When dey got to where dey's goin', Hokey and Big Road Walker took dey rope and got out, but dey made de young'uns and Grandfather Panter and Black Bottom stay in de train and watch from de winders.

Big Road Walker opened de gate to de pasture, and him and Hokey went inside. When dey got inside de pasture, Big Road Walker was in front, and here come a big ole bull, jus' a'gallopin'. Big Road Walker thowed he rope roun' dat ole bull's nake, and he hollered, "I got de bigges' bull dey is. I'se de worl' champion ketchin' bulls. Can't nobody ketch bulls good as I can." And he thowed de bull down and tied he foots together.

Hokey don't say nothin', so he look to see where she is. 'Bout dat time he heared sumpn snortin' and blowin', and he see de bigges', blackes', meanes' bull in de whole worl', makin' at him, and he start to run. Den he laugh and laugh, 'cause dere was Hokey settin' on dat big ole mean bull's haid, and she makin' him ack like he goin' to run over Big Road Walker. While Big Road Walker's makin' all dat fuss 'bout being' de champion bull ketcher Hokey jus' went out and magicked de bigges', blackes', meanes' bull dey was. She have to do things like dat sometime, to keep Big Road Walker from braggin' so much 'bout how good a man he is.

While dey's standin' dere de panter start hollerin', and Hokey say, "Hush you fuss, Big Road Walker, and go let dat panter out so he can stan' behine a tree and beller at de moon. He hollerin' he haid off for you to let him out to holler."

So Big Road Walker go back to de train and let de panter out, but he don't let him go in de pasture where de bulls is at. It's dark down dere in de pasture, but de moon shinin' bright, and ole Grandfather Panter stan' behine a tree and he holler, "Hey, Mr. Moon. What you doin' so far up in de air you can't hear my voice?" And de moon don't say nothin'. Den de panter tell Big Road Walker he's ready to go back on de train, and Big Road Walker tooken him back.

After Big Road Walker tooken de panter back and put him on de train, he went back to de pasture, and he go in, and Hokey's still settin' on dat mean ole bull's haid. Big Road Walker say to her, "Ole lady, how come you can ketch de meanes' bull in de pasture, and I can't?" And Hokey, she say back to him, "Dat's 'cause I'se a magic woman." Den Big Road Walker say, "Why don't you learn me to be magic sometime, 'cause I don't want you follerin' me everywhere I go." Hokey say, "No, I won't learn you to be magic. Bofe of us can't be magic. Dat is too much of a good thing."

"Well," say Big Road Walker, "iffn I can't be magic I reckon we better be gittin' on back home to Newberry wid dis bull. He so big, though, I don't think we goin' to be able to git him thoo dat car box door."

Hokey say she can fix dat all right, and Big

Hokey say, "Now, ole man,
you foller dis train."

Road Walker say, "My wife Hokey, if you do dat for me I be so happy."

So Hokey got down offn dat big ole mean bull's head, and den she thowed up her right han' and she holler, and all de bulls in dat Undergroun' Pasture, and dey's ten thousan' of 'em, come runnin' to her, and stan' still. Big Road Walker say, "What a magic wife I got!"

Den Hokey say, "All of you bulls 'cep' dis one, you go on back to de other en' of de pasture and set down." And dey done it. Den Hokey say, "Dis ole big bull can run jus' as fas' as dis train can run. I'll jus' hol' up my right han' and set at de winder, so's he can see me, and he'll foller de train till we gits home."

Big Road Walker's jus' tickled to deaf to git dat bigges' ole bull to take back home wid him.

When dey got back on de train Hokey set at de winder and hol' up her right han' and pat de bull on de haid and say, "Now, ole man, you foller dis train." And dat ole bull nod he haid and come trottin' longside de train all de way. Hokey keep pattin' dat bull on de haid, and she say, "I'll plant plenty corn for you to eat, so's you won't have to eat jus' ole green grass all de time." And dat ole bull nod he haid again. He can run faster dan dat train, but he don't never git out of sight any time.

He jus' runned long side de train where Hokey's settin', and she keep pattin' him on de haid. Big Road Walker say dat de runninges' bull he ever see.

When dey got back to Newberry, South Cahlina, wid dat bull, dey didn't have no place to put him, so Big Road Walker got out and builded a big ole lot for him to run in. But at night time he go right up outside Hokey's bedroom winder, and she have to sleep wid her han' outside de winder so's she can pat de bull on de haid. He gits lonesome by hisself at night when he don't have no other bulls to run wid.

* 17 *

HOKEY'S SPECIAL PET

One day after Hokey had et her dinner and was settin' restin' her feet, she got to thinkin' and she thunk to herself, "Hokey, here's all dese pets roun' here, and you ain't got no pet dat's jus' yours."

Den she go to fin' Big Road Walker, and he's settin' restin' his feet, but he ain't thinkin', and she say to him, "Ole man, I been thinkin'. Here's all dese pets roun' here, and I ain't got no pet what's jus' mine." And he say, "Dat is a fack. I reckon maybe I git you a pet what's jus' yours when I go walkin' in de woods tonight."

So Big Road Walker went walkin' in de woods dat night, and he's lookin' for a pet what's jus' Hokey's, and he don't know what kind of pet he's goin' to git. He go walkin' long, and he thunk to

[116]

hisself dat 'cause Hokey's so little she have to have a little pet if it be jus' hers.

He look and he look and he look, and he don't fin' no pet. Den he thunk he see a little rabbit hoppin' long, and he say, "Dat de very pet for Hokey," and he go to grab dat rabbit, and it wa'nt no rabbit at all. It were jus' a ole dead stump wid some bushes stickin' up dat looked like ole long rabbit ears.

Den he look some more, and he see a little red fox, and he say, "Dat de very pet for Hokey," and he go to grab dat fox, but dat fox say to him, " 'Scuse me, Mr. Big Road Walker, iffn you please. I ain't got no time to be no pet for Mis' Hokey. I got to go long 'bout my bizness and ketch me sumpn for my babies to eat." And Big Road Walker say all right, he fin' another pet for Hokey.

He look some more, and he seed a little baby deer, and he say, "Dat's de very pet for Hokey." He start to pick up dat baby deer and put him in his poke, but de mama deer and de papa deer see him comin', and dey got dat baby deer and runned so hard dey runned away from Big Road Walker and hid, and he couldn't fin' 'em.

By dat time it's mos' two o'clock in de mornin', and Big Road Walker haven't got no pet for

Hokey. He think maybe he have to go back home and look for a pet tomorrow night.

Bimeby he heared a racket in de bushes, and he heared somebody call him, real weak like. He stop and listen, and somebody say, "Mr. Big Road Walker. Mr. Big Road Walker." He say, "Yes ma'am. Where is you? I hears you but I can't see you." Den he hear de voice say, "Here I is, down in dis pine thicket."

Big Road Walker go over to de pine thicket, and he don't see nobody. He say, "Where at is you in dis pine thicket?" And de voice say, "Here I is, right down here," and he look down, and dere was a little baby lion, 'bout big as a little baby kitten, all curled up on a nice sof' bed of pine needles.

Big Road Walker say, "Baby lion, where is you mama and papa? Is dey gone off and lef' you by youself in dis pine thicket?" And de baby lion say, "My mama and papa got losted from me, and I don't know where dey is. I think I better be your wife Hokey's pet."

So Big Road Walker knowed dat's de very pet for Hokey, and he put dat baby lion in he poke, and he go on home. Dat baby lion had blue eyes and white ears, and a white tail. Big Road Walker say, "Honey, I know my wife Hokey goin' to be proud to have you for her pet."

[118]

Big Road Walker say, "Ole lady, here
is you special pet what's jus' yours."

When Big Road Walker got home it's mos' five o'clock in de mornin', and his folks ain't got up yet. He knock on de door, and Mean O My come and opened it for him. When he see Big Road Walker's got sumpn in he poke, he say, "Daddy, what dat you got?" Big Road Walker say, "I got a baby lion 'bout as big as a little baby kitten, and he got blue eyes and white ears and a white tail." Mean O My say, "Who you goin' to give it to?" And Big Road Walker tole him he got dat baby lion for Mama Hokey's special pet.

Mean O My start to cry 'cause Big Road Walker won't give him dat baby lion, so Big Road Walker say to him, "Son, don't you cry. Dis is Mama Hokey's special pet, but maybe she let you play wid him sometime if you be a good boy."

'Bout dat time Hokey heared 'em talkin', and she come to see what dey's talkin' about. When she come in Big Road Walker say, "Dear wife Hokey, shet you eyes and open you han' and I'll give you sumpn to make you smile."

So she shet her eyes and opened her han', and Big Road Walker put dat baby lion in her han'. When she open her eyes and see dat little baby lion wid blue eyes and white ears and a white tail, she jus' laugh and laugh, she dat proud of him. Big

Road Walker say, "Ole lady, here is you special pet what's jus' yours."

Hokey sot down on de floor by de baby lion, and she say, "What we shall feed dis baby lion to raise him?" And Big Road Walker say, "We feed him fresh meat and sweet milk." She say, "What kin' of bottle we shall git for him?" And Big Road Walker say, "We git him a baby bottle." She say, "What kin' of milk we feed him, cow milk or goat milk?" And Big Road Walker say, "We give him cow milk."

So Big Road Walker go out in de pasture and git him a jersey cow what give five gallons of milk twice a day, and dey raised dat lion till he got to be big as a German police dog. And dat is all de large he got.

Hokey name dat lion Handy Candy, and dat was her special pet.